▲ 世界 500 位傑出名人之一（美國名人傳記），美國 ABI 名人傳記中心，頒給涂秀田二十世紀傑出人物獎，五百位領導人物之一

Outstanding People of the 20th Century
Incorporating the Outstanding Achievement Awards

This is to certify that Tu Shiu-Tien (Sar Po) D.D.S. Litt.D. LFWLA. is included in Outstanding People of the 20th Century in honour of an Outstanding Contribution to Poetry, Childrens Poetry, Dentistry

Signed and Sealed at the International Biographical Centre Cambridge, England

Authorized Officer

16th June 1998
Date

▲ 二十世紀傑出人物獎（英國國際名人傳記中心）

this CERTIFICATE of MERIT
Proclaimed throughout the World

is awarded to

TU SHIU-TIEN (SAR PO) D.D.S LITT.D LFWLA

for

DISTINGUISHED SERVICE

which is the subject of notice
in volume XXVII of the

DICTIONARY OF INTERNATIONAL BIOGRAPHY

Signed & Sealed at the International Biographical Centre,
CAMBRIDGE, ENGLAND.

Date: 12th June 1998

Authorized Officer

Twentieth Century Achievement Award

The Board of Directors of the
American Biographical Institute
sitting in the United States of America
recognizes

Tu Shiu-tien (Sar Po)

as most admirable and
whose career achievements and social contributions
have been selected for permanent documentation in

Five Hundred Leaders of Influence

designed for biographical reference and
inspiration for present-day citizens of the
Twentieth Century as well as future generations.

Registrar

Original Volume of
Five Hundred Leaders of Influence
on Permanent Record and Display at the
U.S. Library of Congress, Washington, D.C.
Publication Date: 1997

▲ 二十世紀傑出人物獎(美國(500位領導人物之一))
英國國際名人傳記中心，頒給淦田(沙白)20世紀傑出人物獎

中國文藝協會文藝獎章證書

（一二）文獎字第○三三號

沙白先生從事詩歌，成績斐然，經推薦評審通過，榮獲本會第六十四屆文藝獎章「文藝工作獎」獎章壹座。

此證

中國文藝協會
全國文藝節慶祝大會

中華民國一〇一二年五月四日

> Saen Sanuk
> The top travel and entertainment magazine in Thailand.
> For advertising call 3911395

THE NATION • SECTION THREE

A rare gathering of poets

By Ann Danalya Usher and Thanong Khanthong

Deluged by an outpouring of words, drowning as we are in the tumultuous babble of mass-communications, the voice of the poet is rarely heard.

Is there a place in a world embracing unbridled outward growth and expansion, for the visionary; for the one who keeps sight of the internal origins of all growth?

The poet whose writing is inspired by Nature is in conflict in the urban technological society. His work becomes a reminiscence — a eulogy to dying Nature, or simple fantasy — an ode to Utopian beauty that no longer exists, and perhaps, never did.

Sar Po of Taiwan: "Poetry ... is clear air.

"The sound of the poet like thunder in the sky will awake the lost modern people. The sound of the poet like the roar of great waves will recall the human primary instinct."

A contingent of more than 300 poets from 40 countries attending the Tenth World Congress of Poets in Bangkok sets as its task to show that poetry can help to bring peace and fraternity to this complicated world.

"The place of poetry in the modern world" is one of the issues Bharathi, who inspired the vision of Indian independence, they said, with words written as long ago as 1921:

We will sing and dance to the tune rustic
Blissful freedom attained so majestic.

They spoke with equal enthusiasm about their own work: "We believe we can do wonders," said one. "We can inspire the people," declared another. "Through poetry we can knit together the unity of the whole world," injected a third.

And who bestows the honour of "poet laureate"? "Society creates the poet master," replied one. "The people choose. We don't bother with the government," retorted another.

"Self-recognition, madame," explained a third, and all of them laughed loudly.

Others at the Congress say that society needs poetry to heal its broken spirituality, and to mend ailing culture. Krishna Srinivas of India, who is president of World Poetry Society Intercontinental, USA, delivered an address to the congress with a fury, celebrating poetry as bringing mankind to redemption and preaching diversity within unity.

"Diversity we have, but along with it we must tolerate changes —

▲ 泰國最大的英文報《The Nation (國民報)》頭版介紹世界詩人大會，開頭就報導沙白 (Sar Po) 的論文。方框處為泰國教授解析沙白論文之精義

TUESDAY, NOVEMBER 15, 1988 • PAGE 25

The youngest voice

Indian-born Oormila Vijayakrishnan is barely 12 years old, yet she is participating the Tenth World Congress of Poets as a mature poet.

A child prodigy, Oormila, who has been living in Kuwait since age three, brings along a collection of her poetry, *Flowers and Butterflies*. It has stolen the show from poets five times her age.

The youngest delegate attending the congress, Oormila has written more than 175 poems, showing a penetrating mind and a keen yearning for beauty and order. She celebrates poetry in a solemn, mystical sense with a mixture of philosophical contemplation.

POETRY
*A mysterious ship of words,
That sails,
to a land,
Unheard......"*

PAST
*The air
In its deceiving stare,
Cuts short the past glories,
Breaking the world of memories.*

She started writing poetry when she was seven years old. "Poetry just comes to me naturally. I can write poetry any time I want to," she says.

Her medium is the English language, though her native tongue is Malayalam, an Indian dialect. Despite her extraordinary gift for poetry, she does not consider herself to be superior to

Oormila

stature, but has a gaze that betrays her 11 years. Her works convey a sincere message of optimism, and of love for her grandfather and brother:

*Grandfather you may have seen,
How wonderful I've been,
Grandfather you may have heard,
   About me your little bird.*

*You thought I'd never write,
But you weren't at all right,
I have written but only after you died,
   But still you are my guide.*

*You are the King of my poetry,
Whatever it might be,*

IX

By the authority of the
United Cultural Convention
sitting in the United States of America

Tu Shiu-Tien

is awarded the

2004
INTERNATIONAL
PEACE PRIZE

*For Outstanding Personal
Achievements to the
Good of Society as a Whole*

Awarded on December 30, 2004

President and General-In-Residence
United Cultural Convention

▲ 涂秀田醫師榮獲英國 ABI 頒發「100 位傑出作家」、「100 位終生成就獎」

▲ 國際世界詩人會 (The intercontinental world poetry society) 頒贈沙白詩作《化粧 (Cosmetice)》卓越獎 (1994 年 7 月 12 日)

This Illuminated Certificate proclaims the induction of

Dr. Tu Shiu-Tien (Sar Po)

into the

Top 100 Writers - 2005

and as such stands testament to the efforts made by said individual in the arena of

Poetry and Literature

Witnessed on the date set out below by the Officers of the International Biographical Centre at its Headquarters in Cambridge, England and signed by the Editor-in-Chief and Director General

Editor-in-Chief

Director General

26th April 2005
Date

Whereas the Director General and the Editorial Board of the International Biographical Centre of Cambridge England have ordered the honouring of the distinguished individual

Dr Shiu-Tien Tu, LFWLA

In that the foreshortened entry posted opposite is included, unabridged, in the prestigious title

"Lifetime of Achievement One Hundred"

published with all due ceremony by the Centre in the year 2005 in order that they may receive recognition both of their achievements and of their contributions to society and to the International Biographical Centre.

Therefore let it be known that by this order the individual is confirmed as an inaugural entrant in Lifetime of Achievement One Hundred. Signed at the Centre's Headquarters in Cambridge, England.

DR SHIU-TIEN TU, LFWLA

Dr Shiu-Tien Tu, also known as Sar Po, is a dentist, poet, writer, translator and publisher. He was born on 28 July 1944 in Taiwan. He married Chiu-chu Tseng on 22 November 1978 and the couple have three children, two sons and a daughter. At Kaohsiung Medical College Dr Tu earned his DDS in 1970. He then undertook postgraduate studies at Osaka Dental University (1972-73), the University of Osaka (1973-74) and at the University of Tokyo (1974-77). In the course of his career he has published several volumes in Chinese and has translated into Chinese the works of T S Eliot, Paul Valery and a number of Japanese writers. As well as contributing to newspapers, reviews, quarterlies and journals he is the author of "Hollow Shells", published in English and Chinese in 1990.

Dr Tu is the winner of the Kaohsiung Literature Prize. He currently holds membership of the following professional organisations: the Chinese Children's Literature Association, the Chinese Literature Association, the Chinese Poets Association, the World Academy of Arts and Culture and the World Chinese Poets Association.

DIRECTOR GENERAL

18th April 2005
DATE

▲ 美國名人傳記頒發給涂秀田世界 500 位傑出名人之一獎

XIII

▲ 世界詩人學會 (World Academy of Arts and Culture) 頒給沙白榮譽文學博士學位

(中英對照)

盛開的詩花

Flowers of Poetry are Blooming

著：沙白
　　Sar Po
譯：陳靖奇教授
　　Ching-chi Chen, Ph.d., Professor Emeritus of English,
　　National Kaohsiung Normal University
封面相片：林景星醫師攝 / 荷花
　　　　　by Dr. Ting-Shing Lin / Lotus

| 序 |　　美麗的花朵，美麗的世界

盛開的詩花

◨ 沙白 撰
　Sar Po
◨ 陳靖奇教授 譯
　Ching-chi Chen, Ph.d.

大自然是美麗的，有美麗的世界

　　我們有美麗的世界，我們有美麗的天空，我們有溫暖的太陽，我們有美麗的月亮，我們有亮晶晶的星星。我們有美麗的山川，我們有綠油油的草原，有美麗的花園，有盛開的花朵。我們有美妙的詩歌，我們有美麗的人生，活著是快樂的，做人是快樂的，我們要珍惜快樂的人生，我們要再創造更美好的世界，享受更美好的人生，生命是可貴的，活著就是幸福。

人類有偉大的愛心和慈悲心。

人類有老子、莊子、孔孟、墨子、佛陀、基督的崇高道德和修養，及慈悲之心，博愛之心。

| Preface | **Beautiful Flowers; Beautiful World**

Flowers of Poetry are Blooming

■ 沙白 撰
　Sar Po
■ 陳靖奇教授 譯
　Ching-chi Chen, Ph.d.

Nature is beautiful and this is a beautiful world.

We have a beautiful world, a beautiful sky, and a warm sun. We have a beautiful moon and shining stars. We have beautiful mountains and rivers. We have green grasslands, beautiful gardens, and blooming flowers. We have beautiful poems. We have beautiful life. To be able to live is happy. Being a human is happy. We should cherish happy life. We want to create a better world and enjoy a better life. Life is precious. Indeed, to be able to live is happiness.

Human beings have great love and compassion.

We have the lofty morality and cultivation of Laozi, Zhuangzi, Confucius and Mencius, Mozi, the Buddha, and the Christ, as well as a heart of compassion and universal love.

・序・美麗的花朵，美麗的世界

人類有像天空一樣，包容天地萬物之心。

人類有像大海一樣，寬大包容之心。

人類有像慈母熱愛子女的偉大愛心。

有男女戀情之愛心。

有夫妻恩愛之愛心，有人間互愛互助的熱情和良心。

有子女孝順父母的孝心。

盛開的詩花

有美麗的花朵

展開可愛的笑容，和蝴蝶擁吻

和我們一起歡樂

這是一個美麗的世界

　　　　可愛的世界

　　　　幸福的世界

這是大家的世界

讓我們共同愛護這個世界

使它成為永久美麗的世界

Preface · Beautiful Flowers; Beautiful World

Human beings have a heart that embraces everything in the world like the sky.
Human beings have a heart of generosity and tolerance like the ocean.
Human beings have a great love as a loving mother loves her children.
There is love between men and women.
There is the conjugal love between husband and wife, and the enthusiasm and conscience of mutual love and mutual assistance in the world.
There is the filial piety of children to obey their parents.
Flowers of poetry are blooming.
There are beautiful flowers everywhere.
The flowers smile and embrace the butterflies.
They are having fun with us.
It is a beautiful world.
It is a lovely world.
It should be a happy world.
The world belongs to everybody.
Let us love this world together and
Make it a beautiful world forever.

目錄 Table of Content

- 002 序/美麗的花朵，美麗的世界
  Preface/Beautiful Flowers; Beautiful World
- 006 目錄
  Table of Content
- 010 蝴蝶不來，花朵也開
  If Butterflies Did Not Come, Flowers Would Still Bloom
- 012 兩支筷子
  Two Chopsticks
- 016 妳想變成什麼花
  What Flower Do You Want to be
- 020 孤獨的故鄉小河
  How Lonely My Hometown River Is
- 022 春天一定會來
  Spring Will Surely Arrive
- 026 爬一座山，寫一首詩
  Climbing a Mountain and Writing a Poem
- 030 一滴水
  A Drop of Water
- 034 我的內心有個美麗的花園
  There is a Beautiful Garden in My Heart
- 036 山上的搖籃
  A Cradle Between the Mountains
- 038 春天永遠住在我們心裡
  Spring Will Always Live in our Hearts
- 040 花園的萬朵花是萬首詩
  Ten Thousand Flowers in a Garden are Ten Thousand Poems
- 042 芳香的木蘭花是一首詩
  The Fragrant Magnolia is a Poem
- 044 快樂的雲朵帶我到天上
  Happy Clouds Would Take Me to the Sky
- 046 心中有花園
  There is a Garden in One's Heart
- 048 坐在雲朵上
  Sitting on a Cloud
- 050 月亮就是妳
  The Moon is You
- 052 微笑是最美麗的風景
  Smile is the Most Beautiful Scenery
- 054 天總會亮
  It Will Always be Bright in the Sky
- 056 時間易飛逝
  Time Flies
- 058 太陽是孤單的
  The Sun is Alone
- 062 問星星幸福在哪裡
  Let us Ask the Stars Where Happiness is
- 064 用心觸美最美
  The Beauty that Touches One's Heart is the Most Beautiful.
- 068 人生如鐵
  Life Can Be Compared to Iron
- 070 我們是大海裡的一滴水
  Each One of us is like a Drop of Water in the Sea
- 072 詩風吹動人心
  Let the Wind of Poetry Move the Heart
- 074 太陽讀懂黑夜
  The Sun Understands the Night

· Table of Content ·

076	願我是一隻飛鳥 I Wish that I were a Bird Flying High in the Sky		106	每一朵花都有存在的理由 Every Flower Has a Reason to Exist
078	讓往事隨風飄去 Let the Past Go with the Wind		108	不帶刺的詩 Poetry without Thorns
080	春燕飛入我心 A Swallow in Spring Flew into my Heart		110	寫在河流的詩 Poems Written on the River
082	詩意的風 The Poetic Wind		112	我的詩隨彩雲飛揚 I Wish that my Poems Would Fly with the Colorful Clouds
084	我喝著月光酒 I Drink Moonlight Wine		114	讓我們的憂愁交給河流 Let us Hand our Sorrows over to the River
086	手握時間 Seize the Day		116	花美花香花悅耳 Flowers are Beautiful, Fragrant and Melodious
088	落葉悲秋 Fallen Leaves in Sad Autumn		118	詩歌插在雲雀的翅膀 If We Inserted Poetry on a Lark's Wings
090	故鄉的河流唱著歌 The River of my Hometown Sings		120	美麗芬芳的花朵擁抱陽光 Beautiful, Fragrant Flowers are Embracing the Sun
092	醉人的黃昏 Twilight that is Intoxicating		122	一隻可愛的雲雀 A Cute Lark
094	我打碎了中秋月亮 I Broke the Mid-Autumn Moon in Pieces		124	把我們的詩交給鳥兒歌唱 Let us Give our Poems to the Birds to Sing
096	莊嚴思索的大山 The Mountain of Solemn Contemplation		126	不要吹熄別人的燈火 Don't Blow out Other People's Lights
098	我每天微笑著生活 I Live with Smiles Every Day		128	我是一隻雲雀 I Wish I were a Lark
100	天上的星星是我們的眼睛 The Stars in the Sky are our Eyes		130	讓悲傷隨落葉飄走 Let Sadness Drift Away with Fallen Leaves
102	還你一湖水 I Shall Return a Lake of Water to You		132	把生活變成詩 Let us Turn Life into Poetry
104	喝了美酒的夕陽 The Sun at Dusk Seemed to Have Been Drunk			

Flowers of Poetry are Blooming   007

·目錄·

134	把自己當鑽石磨亮 Polish Yourself like a Diamond		166	憂鬱的月亮 The Sad Moon
136	相逢是首詩 Meeting is a Poem		168	有翅膀的夢想 Dreams with Wings
138	酸甜苦辣都是詩 Ups and Downs in Life Could be Poetry		170	妳是人間最美的情歌 You are the Most Beautiful Love Song in the World
140	微笑是最美麗的語言 Smile is the Most Beautiful Language		172	我們的愛情堅若鑽石 Our Love Is as Firm as a Diamond
142	我們生活在詩的世界裡 We Live in a World of Poetry		174	傾斜的郵筒 A Slanted Postbox
144	花好月圓 A Full Moon and Good Flowers		176	叩頭須要叩到泥土裡 If One Kowtows, One Has to Do So as to Touch the Dirt
146	像月亮一樣的愛 Parents' Love is like the Light of the Moon		178	用愛畫妳 Drawing a Picture of You with Love
148	我打碎了夕陽 I Wish to Break Down the Sunset into Pieces		180	我是高山 I Wish that I Were a High Mountain
150	雲是天上的飛鳥 Clouds are Birds in the Sky		182	愛是一條河 Love is like a River
152	星星是天上的明珠 Stars Are Pearls in the Sky		184	多情的花 Amorous Flowers
154	明天的天空會更蔚藍 I Wish that the Sky Tomorrow Would be Bluer		186	月餅 Mooncakes
156	月亮為你歌唱 I Wish that the Moon Would Sing for You		188	一朵美麗的花 A Beautiful Flower
158	雲給月亮蓋上了棉被 The Cloud Covers the Moon with a Quilt		190	初秋的落葉 Fallen Leaves in Early Autumn
160	像美酒的詩獻給月亮 I Wish to Dedicate Wine-like Poetry to the Moon		192	花兒笑什麼 Why Is the Flower Smiling
162	家是天堂 The Home is Like Paradise		194	像雨一樣的淚水 Tears Drop like Rain Showers

Table of Content

196	台灣美酒灌醉了太陽 Let the Sun Get Drunk with Taiwan' Wine		226	憂鬱的雲 A Melancholic cloud
198	喝醉的雨 The Rain that Has Been Drunk		228	彩雲追月 Colored Clouds Pursuing the Moon
200	綿綿情歌飛翔雲間 Love Songs Flying in the Clouds		230	彎彎的河流載著我的淚水 The Curved River Carries My Tears.
202	愛是最美的風景 Love Is the Most Beautiful Scenic Spot		232	做天梯爬上月亮 I Wish to Build a Ladder Leading to the Moon.
204	我是天上的雲朵 If I Were a Cloud in the Sky		234	月亮守在妳的窗外 The Moon is Waiting Outside Your Window
206	海的大肚量 The Sea Has a Huge Capacity		236	流淚的飛蛾(一) A Weeping Moth (I)
208	白雲飄著我的詩想 The White Cluods Are Carrying My Poetry		238	流淚的飛蛾(二) A Tearful Moth (II)
210	天上有很多星星是我們的眼睛 I Wish that the Many Stars in the Sky Would Be Our Eyes		240	星星是我的眼睛 The Stars Are My Eyes
212	海是我的愛人 The Sea Is My Sweetheart		242	我有兩支翅膀 If I Had Two Wings
214	上弦月之吻 A Kiss from the First Quarter Moon		244	哭泣的風 The Weeping Wind
216	七夕情歌 Love Songs on te Chiness Valentine's Day		246	春天從大武山出發 Spring Starts from Mount Dawu
218	情人像甜美的月亮 My Sweetheart Is Like the Beautiful Moon		248	春天從大武山出發 Spring Starts from Mount Dawu
220	陳年的相思酒 Aged wine of Lovesickness		250	摘下月亮 Picking the Moon
222	愛是花的芳香 Love is Like Flower's Fragrance		252	作者‧沙白簡介 An Introduction to Tu Shiu-tien (Sar Po)
224	聽醉人的歌聲 Songs that Are Intoxicating		260	譯者‧陳靖奇簡介 Translated by Prof. Ching-chi Chen, Ph.d.

Flowers of Poetry are Blooming

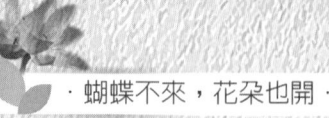

📖 蝴蝶不來，花朵也開

開花是花木生命的展現
蝴蝶不來
花朵也開
花朵盛開
花木的生命就燦爛
花香撲鼻
蝴蝶聞香
就會從近遠飛來
沒有讀者
詩人照樣寫詩
寫了一篇又一篇的美妙好詩
感人心底
就會有一群讀者來朗讀
朗誦不停
就會傳遍萬里

📖 If Butterflies Did Not Come, Flowers Would Still Bloom

Flowering is the display of the life of flowers and trees.
If butterflies did not come,
Flowers would still bloom.
They would still bloom wildly.
The wildly blooming would indicate the strong life of flower trees.
There would be floral fragrance which
Butterflies, far and near,
Would come to smell.
On the other hand, if there were no readers around,
The poet would still write poems.
He would still write one wonderful poem after another.
The poems he writes might appeal to his potential readers.
There would be a group of readers to read them aloud.
The poems might be recited on and on, and
They would spread thousands of miles in the world.

· 兩支筷子 ·

📖 兩支筷子

一支筷子
青菜豆腐夾不到
大魚大肉也夾不到
只有眼睛看得到
嘴巴也吃不到
只有父親
沒有母親
或者
只有母親
沒有父親
都是破碎的家庭
像夾不到菜
　夾不到肉的
單支筷子
享受不到口福
也沒有家庭的幸福
父母像一雙筷子

📖 Two Chopsticks

An only chopstick
Cannot pick up green vegetables and tofu,
Nor can it pick up fish and meat.
One can see the food with eyes, and
One's mouth cannot eat it.
If there is only father and
No mother,
Or
Only mother and
No father in the family,
It is a broken family.
It is like an only chopstick with which
One could not pick up meat.
With an only chopstick,
One cannot enjoy the taste of food.
It is the same with the happiness of the family.
Parents are like a pair of chopsticks.

· 兩支筷子 ·

要永遠在一起
才有功能，才有福氣
我們要孝順父母
讓全家團圓和氣
才是做人的道理

· Two Chopsticks ·

They should be together all the time.

With the two together, the family would function well and there would be happiness.

We have to pay filial piety to our parents.

Only in such a situation can we enjoy the happiness and togetherness of the family.

This is how we might be good members of the family.

· 妳想變成什麼花 ·

📖 妳想變成什麼花

妳想變成牡丹花
給人雍容華貴的氣氛
給人國泰平安的富裕
妳想變成夜來香
給人工作忙碌了一天
好好聞香休息
妳想變成杏花
釀成杏花酒
甜甜蜜蜜
給李白喝完酒後
多寫幾首詩
妳想變成向日葵
吸取了陽光能量
散發給我們快樂和營養
妳可以像孫悟空
七十二變為多種花
給蝴蝶採蜜

What Flower Do You Want to be

You might want to be a peony to
Give a graceful and luxurious atmosphere,
Peace and prosperity to people.
You might want to be night-blooming jasmine
Which would give fragrance to people having worked through a busy day.
They would then take a good rest.
You might want to become apricot blossom which
Would be used to brew apricot wine.
It is sweet wine which
Li Po would drink.
He would then write many poems.
You might want to be a sunflower which
Would absorb energy from the sun
Giving happiness and nourishment to us.
You are truly like The Monkey
With whose seventy-two turns you could turn yourself into many kinds of flowers.
The butterflies would taste your honey and

· 妳想變成什麼花 ·

給人歡喜
女人女人可以變成很多花
給世界美麗
給男人活氣
是人類的福氣

· What Flower Do You Want to be ·

Give joy to people.
Woman! Woman! You could also become many flowers
To give beauty to the world and
Cheer up a man.
It would be the blessing of mankind!

· 孤獨的故鄉小河 ·

📖 孤獨的故鄉小河

熟悉的故鄉小河
離別了多年
因為孤獨
愈來愈瘦小
孤獨的小河
請別憂愁
我會常回來散步，看你
和你一起唱歌
我愛你
讓我擁抱你
把你擁抱到
我住的城市裡
早晚看著你，照顧你
永遠陪著你
使你不再孤獨

📖 How Lonely My Hometown River Is

My hometown river, which used to be familiar to me,
Has haunted me because I have been away for many years.
He has become lonesome and
Gotten thinner and thinner.
Lonely river!
Please don't worry.
I would often come back to see you and take a walk along you.
I would sing with you.
I love you!
Let me hug you.
I would take you to
The city where I live.
There, I would take care of you and watch you day and night.
I would always be with you, and
You would never be lonely any longer.

📖 春天一定會來

爬完了山坡
下來就是平地
下完了冬雪
就是溫暖的春天
　　美麗的春天
辛苦工作之後
就有了快樂的收穫
沒有冰冷的冬天
就沒有溫和宜人的春天
人生是一個起伏的波浪
有起有伏
像薛西佛斯推巨石
週而復始
永不休止
沒有平靜無波浪的人生
生命是一場起伏的波浪
當波浪興起時

📖 Spring Will Surely Arrive

One who has finished climbing the mountain
Would come down to the flat ground.
After winter snow is over,
The warm spring would arrive.
It is the beautiful spring.
Having worked hard,
One would harvest happy crops.
If there were no cold winter,
No mild and pleasant spring would ensue.
Life is full of surfs and waves.
There are ups and downs.
It is like Sisyphus' pushing the boulder up the mountain.
The boulder would come down—
Repeatedly and endlessly up and down.
There is no calm and waveless life.
Life is full of surfs and waves.
When the waves rise,

我們就要衝鋒破浪
跨越波浪
創造豐富的人生
我們要征服慘酷的冬天
創造更美好的春天

· Spring Will Surely Arrive ·

We should ride the waves and
Conquer the waves.
What we need is to create a rich life.
We have to conquer the harsh winter and
Create a better spring.

📖 爬一座山，寫一首詩

我們要爬一座山
寫一首詩
把詩放在山頂上
一座山有一條生命
我們的詩也有了生命
有了豐富生命的詩
可以使地球充滿活力
當一萬個詩人
爬過萬座山時
就有萬首詩在山頂上
滿山都是用紅紙寫的詩
這是萬山詩的世界
太陽看了
供給燦爛的陽光
照耀詩篇
詩象萬千
月亮看了萬山詩

📖 Climbing a Mountain and Writing a Poem

I am going to climb a mountain and
Write a poem.
I want to put the poem on top of a mountain.
The mountain has a life;
My poem also has a life.
The poem which has a full life
Could rejuvenate the earth.
When ten thousand poets
Have climbed ten thousand mountains,
There would be ten thousand poems on top of the mountains.
The mountains would be full of poems written on red paper.
This is a world of the mountains of ten thousand poems.
The sun who sees this
Would provide bright sunshine
Making the poems shine.
The poems would be in various shapes.
When the moon sees the poems,

覺得好奇
就下來跟我們吟詩遊戲
星星也下來一起唱萬家詩
大家都很快樂,很和氣

She would feel curious and

Come down to chant the poems and play with us.

The stars would also come down and chant the poems together.

Everyone would be happy and be at peace with everyone else.

📖 一滴水

一滴水
是一個生命
一滴水
有圓滿的生命
當一滴水將要枯乾時
就要投入海中
就可以好好存活
我們的生命
就是一滴水
要好好珍惜這滴水
不要浪費,不要虛耗
讓這滴水
像一顆不滅的鑽石
永遠亮麗
永不腐朽,永不枯乾
我們要變成像鑽石一樣的水
變成完美的人

📖 A Drop of Water

A drop of water is entitled to
A life.
A drop of water should
Enjoy a full life.
When a drop of water is about to dry up,
It is expected to end up in the sea
Where it could survive.
Our life is
Like a drop of water.
We should cherish this drop of water.
We should not waste it, nor should we throw it away.
This drop of water is
Like a diamond which would endure eternally.
The drop of water, like the diamond, would always be bright.
It will never decay, nor will it become dry.
I wish that we should be like the drop of water which is like a diamond.
We should perfect ourselves

變成永恆的人
變成千秋萬世
永垂不朽的人

And become eternal and
Live forever.
In short, we should be like an immortal man.

📖 我的內心有個美麗的花園

世態炎涼
戰火連綿
而我的內心有個美麗的花園
是八十億人的世外桃源
可以供大家避難的大花園
歡迎大家來欣賞遊玩
給我們終生安樂享天年

📖 There is a Beautiful Garden in My Heart

The world is full of ups and downs.
There are endless wars.
Yet, there is a beautiful garden in my heart.
It might be a paradise for eight billion people.
It could be a large garden where everyone could take refuge.
Everyone is welcome to loiter in it.
The garden might enable one to enjoy a life of joy and peace.

📖 山上的搖籃

我坐在兩山間的搖籃上
搖啊!搖啊!搖
搖到山頂上
山頂上有個漂亮的月亮姑娘
我要抓住月亮
放在搖籃上
陪我一起搖蕩
　　一起歌唱
它帶我到天上
帶到快樂天堂

📖 A Cradle Between the Mountains

I sit on a cradle between two mountains.
Swing and swing!
I swing to the top of the mountains.
There is a beautiful girl, the moon, on the top.
I want to catch the moon and
Place her on the cradle
To swing with me.
We would sing together.
She would take me to the sky and
To the happy heaven.

📖 春天永遠住在我們心裡

我們不要夏天、秋天和冬天
春天永遠住在我們的心裡
滿園的香花開在我們心裡
鳥兒也在我們心裡歌唱
滿園都是快樂的蜜蜂
採擷甜蜜的花汁
供我們吸食
天堂就在這裡
天堂就在永遠住著春天的心裡

📖 Spring Will Always Live in our Hearts

We don't want summer, autumn or winter.
What we need is spring which will always live in our hearts.
There is a garden full of fragrant flowers in our hearts.
Birds sing in our hearts, too.
The garden is full of happy bees
Sucking sweet flower juice
For us to eat.
Heaven is here.
Heaven is in the heart where spring always lives.

📖 花園的萬朵花是萬首詩

我們有很多詩
花園的萬朵花就是萬首詩
每朵花都很芳香
很美麗
每首詩都很芳香
很美麗
我們都可以徜徉在花叢間
像蜜蜂一樣
吸取芳香甜蜜的花汁
給你舒服
又像讀三百首唐詩
吸取名詩的精華
給我們心靈充實
無限舒暢
而我們寫的詩
要像芳香美麗的花朵
人人喜愛
愛不忍釋
傳誦千里

📖 Ten Thousand Flowers in a Garden are Ten Thousand Poems

We have many poems.
Ten thousand flowers in a garden are ten thousand poems.
Every flower is fragrant and
Beautiful.
Likewise, every poem is fragrant and
Beautiful.
We can all wander among the flowers in the garden
Like bees.
We can drink the sweet and fragrant flower juice, which would
Make us comfortable.
It is like reading three hundred Tang poems.
We absorb the essence of famous poems to
Enrich our souls.
We would enjoy unlimited comfort in reading them.
The poems we write
Are like fragrant and beautiful flowers
Which we would enjoy and
We would not give them up.
The poems would be read by people far and wide.

📖 芳香的木蘭花是一首詩

芳香的木蘭花樹
長在美麗的庭院裡
白天吸取太陽的能量
晚上吸取精華的夜光
木蘭花開滿樹
木蘭花香溢四方
我們的詩寫在木蘭花上
芳香的花
使我們的詩也芳香
芳香的花揚千里
芳香的詩傳萬里
使我們的身體芳香
我們的心也芳香
整個世界都是美麗芳香

📖 The Fragrant Magnolia is a Poem

The magnolia tree is full of fragrance.
It is growing in a beautiful garden.
It absorbs the energy of the sun during the day and
The essence of the nightly glory in the evening.
The magnolia is in full blossom.
The fragrance of it spreads everywhere.
My poems are written on magnolias flowers.
They are fragrant, which
Also makes my poems fragrant.
Fragrant flowers spread thousands of miles, and
Equally, fragrant poems spread thousands of miles.
They make our bodies smell perfume.
They also make our hearts fragrant.
The whole world is beautiful and fragrant.

📖 快樂的雲朵帶我到天上

快樂的雲朵
看見我一個人在地球上很孤獨
帶我到天上
一起唱歌
一起跳舞
它說不要只在地球上寫詩
也要到天上寫詩
寫給太陽、月亮、星星欣賞
寫給太空人欣賞
大家都快樂，喜氣洋洋

📖 Happy Clouds Would Take Me to the Sky

Happy clouds,
Seeing me alone and lonely on earth,
Would like to take me to the sky.
We would sing together and
Dance together there.
They advise me against just writing poetry on earth.
They suggest that I should also write poetry in the sky.
I should write to the sun, the moon, and stars.
I should write for the astronauts to read.
There in the sky, everyone would be happy and smiling.

📖 心中有花園

每個人心中都有一座花園
一座美麗的花園
天天去灌溉施肥
就會滿園花開
你不管它
就會荒蕪，雜草叢生
我們要修心養性
心裡就會開花
其樂無窮
人生無限光明

📖 There is a Garden in One's Heart

There should be a garden in everyone's heart.
In the beautiful garden,
One has to irrigate and fertilize every day.
It will be full of flowers.
If one does not take care of it,
It will be barren and weeds will grow.
In the same manner, one needs to cultivate one's mind.
Like the garden, there will be flowers in one's heart.
With the flowers, it will be fun.
Life would be infinitely bright.

📖 坐在雲朵上

我坐在雲朵上
像騎在千里馬背上
天馬行空
逍遙自在
又像一隻巨鵬
在高空飛翔
展現凌雲之壯志
顯露傲視天下之高貴氣息
真是不可一世

📖 Sitting on a Cloud

I sit on a cloud as if
I were riding on the back of a horse that travels one thousand miles
In an unconstrained manner.
I am carefree
Like a giant roc.
I seem to be able to fly high
Showing the lofty ambition and
Revealing my proud, noble vision.
It is really awesome being there.

📖 月亮就是妳

我每天看著漂亮的月亮
月亮就是妳
月亮也看著我
月亮也看著妳
妳像月亮一樣漂亮
愈看愈漂亮
我愛月亮
月亮也愛我
我愛妳
妳也愛我
心心相印
心心相連
我擁抱著月亮
月亮也擁抱著我
我抱妳
妳抱我
這是演不完的
愛的圓舞曲

The Moon is You

I look at the beautiful moon every day.
The moon is you.
The moon is watching me, and
The moon is watching you, too.
You are as beautiful as the moon.
The more I look at you, the more beautiful you are.
I love the moon, and
The moon loves me, too.
I love you, the moon, and I believe that
You love me, too.
We are linked heart to heart and again
Mind to mind.
I like to hug the moon, and
The moon is happy to embrace me, too.
I hug you, and
You hug me.
It is an endless play of
The waltz of love.

📖 微笑是最美麗的風景

最美麗的風景對我們微笑
我們的微笑是最美麗的風景
微笑使美麗的風景更美麗
美麗的風景使微笑更可愛
微笑一開
美麗的風景就燦爛展開
微笑常開
美麗的風景常在
微笑是我們的財富
有了微笑，我們就擁有
更大更美的風景區
我們就擁有更大更美的財富

📖 Smile is the Most Beautiful Scenery

The most beautiful scenery is its smiling at us.
Our smile is the most beautiful scenery.
Smile makes the scenery more beautiful.
The beautiful scenery makes the smile more lovely.
Once one keeps smiling,
The beautiful scenery would be brilliant.
Where there is smile,
There will always be beautiful sceneries.
Truly, smile is our wealth.
Truly, wealth comes with a smile.
We shall have bigger and more beautiful scenic spots.
Indeed, we shall have bigger and better wealth.

📖 天總會亮

不可能天天都黑夜
天總會亮
一定會出現陽光
就像胎兒一定會誕生
新生的一代
一定會出現
每天都會產生新的希望
人生沒有永久的痛苦
也沒有永久的悲傷
人人生而平等
抬頭仰望天空
人人都可以看見
美麗的陽光
陽光會趕走黑夜
陽光會消除霉氣
給我們巨大能量
給我們無限的希望

📖 It Will Always be Bright in the Sky

It can't be night all the time.
It will always be bright.
There will surely be sunshine.
A fetus is bound to be born, and
A new generation
Will definitely appear.
Every day brings a new hope.
Life is not always full of eternal pain,
Nor is it full of permanent sorrow.
All men are created equal.
As long as one looks up at the sky,
One can see
The beautiful sunshine.
The sun will drive away night.
Sunshine will take away the mildew, and
Give us great both energy and
Infinite hope.

📖 時間易飛逝

時間易飛逝
一眨眼就消失
一過目
幾個春秋就離去
哀傷也不能追回
我們只有寫詩
用詩抓住時間的尾巴
不讓它溜走
讓時間變成我們的好朋友
跟我們一起遊戲
不會離去
不會飛走

📖 Time Flies

Time flies and
Disappears in the blink of an eye
At a glance,
Years pass by
Leaving no traces of sadness of the old days.
What we can do is write poetry
To catch the tail of time.
We would not let it slip away;
Instead, we should make friends with it and
Play with it.
We would not part with each other.
We believe that it would not fly away.

太陽是孤單的

太陽高掛在天空上
太陽是孤單的
但是,它卻不寂寞
因為它放出光芒給人類
人類就成為它的好朋友
它不會寂寞
因為它慷慨施捨它的熱能
賜給我們生命
給我們溫暖
給我們舒服
它不會孤單
因為付出了不回報的慈善
讓我們感激
使我們成為它的好朋友
永遠在一起
它比聖誕老人還慈祥
它不是給我們糖果吃

The Sun is Alone

The sun is high in the sky.
The sun is alone,
But he is not lonely.
He shines on mankind.
Human beings become his good friends.
He won't be lonely
Because he gives heat generously.
He gives us life.
He gives us warmth and
Makes us comfortable.
He won't be alone
For having given us unrequited charity.
We must be grateful to him.
Let us make good friends with him.
Let us get together with him forever.
He is kinder than Santa Claus
Not for giving us candies

· 太陽是孤單的 ·

而是給我們熱能和光芒
所以它是我們最尊敬的好朋友
它有八十億個朋友
跟它一起遊戲
永遠不會孤寂

· The Sun is Alone ·

But for giving us heat and light.
He is our most respected good friend.
He has eight billion friends who like to
Play with him.
He would never be lonely.

📖 問星星幸福在哪裡

我翻山越嶺
爬上玉山頂
問閃亮的星星
你們幸福不幸福
它們回答說很幸福
因為沒有人類的噪雜聲
所以很清淨,很幸福
我抓住星星的尾巴
飛到天上旅行
覺得很幸福

星星說
你如果能在天上朗讀你優美的詩
讓太陽、月亮、星星都聽到
就會更幸福
於是,我就讀了我的詩
讓我和星星、月亮、太陽都很幸福
原來幸福就在我們的心中和詩裡

📖 Let us Ask the Stars Where Happiness is

I went over the mountains.
I climbed Mount Jade.
I asked the shining stars:
"Are you happy or not?"
They answered that they were happy
Because there were no human noises in the sky
So everything there was clean and happy.
I grabbed the tail of the stars and
Flew to the sky.
I felt very happy there.

The stars say that
If you could read your beautiful poems in the sky
To the sun, the moon, and the stars,
They will be happy.
So I read my poems
To please the stars, the moon, the sun and myself.
It turns out that happiness lies in our hearts and poems.

📖 用心觸美最美

用眼睛看了一朵美花
覺得很美
那是表象的美
要觸動心弦的美
才是真美
要內心覺得必須吸入其深深的美味
才過癮的美
才是真美

也像欣賞一首美妙的歌曲
不是表面上覺得好聽而已
而是要震撼在心裡
在心裡繚繞多次
才會生出真正的美味
這才是真美

📖 The Beauty that Touches One's Heart is the Most Beautiful.

I see a beautiful flower with my eyes and
Feel its beauty.
That is a superficial beauty.
Beauty that is approached with one's heart
Is a true one.
To be touched inwardly is to taste its deepest deliciousness.
That is a beauty one would be attracted to.
It is a true beauty.

Likewise, it is like listening to a beautiful song.
One is not merely touched by it on the surface,
But shocked at heart.
The melody would be wandering in one's heart over and over again.
The real deliciousness would be felt.
That is a true beauty.

又像欣賞一首絕妙的詩
不只看它意境高，詩詞美
而是要看它對內心的感觸有多深
才是真正的好詩
真正美好的詩
不會褪色
不會消失
永久亮麗

The Beauty that Touches One's Heart is the Most Beautiful.

Moreover, it is like reading a wonderful poem.

One not only looks at how its artistic wording is used to construct the beautiful poem

But also how deeply one feels about it at heart.

Only by this way can one really read a good poem,

A beautiful poem.

The poem will not fade.

It would not disappear and

Would remain bright forever.

人生如鐵

人生如鐵
天天生活
天天錘鍊
由鐵砂錘煉成生鐵
由生鐵錘煉成硬鋼
都歷經過熊熊烈火
才能成為堅硬的純鋼
軟弱的人生
消極的人生
要經過烈火錘鍊
日夜磨練
才能成為頂天立地的英雄好漢

Life Can Be Compared to Iron

Life can be compared to iron.
We live our life every day, and
We should receive challenges every day.
Pig iron is forged from iron sand and
Steel, from pig iron.
Iron has to go through a raging fire
To become hard pure steel.
In the same manner, a weak man, or more aptly,
A negative man,
Should be tempered by challenges,
Day and night,
To become an indomitable hero.

· 我們是大海裡的一滴水 ·

📖 我們是大海裡的一滴水

我們是大海裡的一滴水
我們是晶瑩剔透的一滴水
像閃爍在大海裡的一顆鑽石
鮮活亮麗
閃閃發亮
我們的生命雖然渺小
都有像大海一樣的毅力
和大海一樣勇敢的怒吼勇氣
展現詩的美妙力量
發揚宇宙的真理
發揚宇宙的正義
這是不怕海洋吞食的一滴水
永恆不滅一滴水

📖 Each One of us is like a Drop of Water in the Sea

Each one of us is like a drop of water in the sea.
We are all crystal clear drops of water
Like diamonds shining in the sea,
Fresh and bright,
Brilliantly shining.
Even though our lives are small,
We are as perseverant as the sea.
We are as brave as the sea in roaring,
Demonstrating the wonderful power of poetry,
Promoting the truth of the universe and
Promoting justice in the universe.
This is a drop of water not afraid of being swallowed by the ocean.
This is an everlasting drop of water.

📖 詩風吹動人心

風會吹動花草
讓花草快樂跳舞
展示生命的奧秘
展現生命的活力
願詩風吹動人心
豐富我們的心靈
震撼我們的心靈
讓詩風吹滿整個世界
讓我們穿著風衣
到處飛揚
四處遊戲
使人人愛詩
人人歌唱
隨詩風起舞
世界充滿和樂歡喜

📖 Let the Wind of Poetry Move the Heart

Wind moves flowers so that
Flowers and plants dance happily
Showing the secret and
The vitality of life.
May the wind of poetry move people's hearts and
Enrich their hearts.
May the wind of poetry shock our hearts.
Let the wind of poetry further move the whole world.
Let us wear overcoats with which
We would fly everywhere.
We would play around.
We would make everyone love poetry so much that
Everyone would sing and
Dance with poetry.
I would like to see the world full of joy and peace.

📖 太陽讀懂黑夜

太陽讀懂黑夜
就像生命讀懂死亡
黑夜只是白天的休息
死亡也是生命的休息
黑夜讓太陽睡眠
死亡讓生命超度延續
黑夜讓太陽充電
使充滿活力
照亮溫暖我們的大地
都是大道的輪迴
都是宇宙不滅的天理

📖 The Sun Understands the Night

The sun understands the night,
Just as life understands death.
The night is only the time for the day to rest.
Death is also rest for life.
The night puts the sun to sleep.
Death, on the other hand, is life's reincarnation.
The night charges the sun
To gain energy.
The sun lights up and warms our earth.
It's all about the Way of reincarnation.
It's all about the immortality of the universe

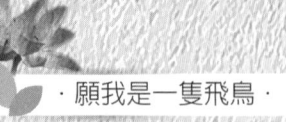

📖 願我是一隻飛鳥

願我是一隻飛鳥
從東飛到西
從南飛到北
從這一山飛到那一山
遊過許多江山
飛過萬重山
飛過萬里路
勝讀萬卷書
白天快樂的遊山玩水
晚上摘星追月
不亦樂乎
你振翅一飛
世間就充滿快樂的喜氣
增加人生的生活樂趣

📖 I Wish that I were a Bird Flying High in the Sky

I wish that I were a bird flying high in the sky.
I would fly from east to west and
From south to north.
I would fly from mountain to mountain.
I would roam among rivers and mountains.
Indeed, I would fly over the mountains and
Cover thousands of miles.
It is said that doing so would surpass reading thousands upon thousands of books.
I would be happy traveling around in the daytime and
Chasing the moon and stars at night.
Truly, I would be happy.
Spread your wings and fly!
The world is full of joy and bliss.
Roaming and flying around would give me the joy of life.

📖 讓往事隨風飄去

讓往事隨風飄去
飄走到遙遠遙遠的地方去
讓我們看不到,找不到
連風的尾巴都抓不到
讓我們不再追憶
不再走黑暗的舊路
我們要走的是光明大道
我們要的是活在精彩美好的今天
我們要的是追求未來幸福美滿的明天

📖 **Let the Past Go with the Wind**

Let the past go with the wind.
Let it float to far away places,
Where we cannot see it, nor can we find it.
It would not even be caught by the tail of the wind.
We shall not remember it.
We would not take the dark old road anymore.
What we would do is to go on a bright road.
What we would do is to live a wonderful and beautiful day today.
What we would do is to pursue a happy and prosperous future.

📖 春燕飛入我心

美麗的春天
可愛的燕子
快樂的飛來飛去
牠飛入我心
　訴我
春花盛開的美好日子
已經來臨
牠帶我四處遊樂飛行
享受人生最大的樂趣

📖 A Swallow in Spring Flew into my Heart

It was beautiful spring.
A cute swallow
Flew here and there.
It flew into my heart.
It told me
That the beautiful day in spring when flowers were fully blooming
Had arrived.
The swallow then took me flying around for fun
To enjoy the greatest joy in life.

· 詩意的風 ·

📖 詩意的風

詩意的風很涼爽
詩意的風,來自海上
智者樂海
使你的胸襟開朗
深悟人生的大道理
詩意的風,來自山上
仁者樂山
樂於深藏山之堅守義理
樂於擁抱山的堅強義氣
詩意的風,來自田園
使我們快樂的
徜徉於無際的綠油油鄉間
詩意的風,吹著吹著
讓李白的酒喝著,喝著
　李白的詩寫著,寫著
使我們渾身沾滿濃濃的李白詩意
使世界更洋溢著詩情樂趣

📖 The Poetic Wind

The poetic wind is cool.
It might be from the sea.
The wise man is happy with the sea.
The poetic wind which is from the sea makes us open-minded.
It helps us understand the truth of life.
The poetic wind, however, might come from the mountains.
The benevolent man tends to love the mountains.
There, we would be happy to delve into the principles hidden deeply in the mountains.
We would be happy to embrace the strong spirit of loyalty of the mountains.
The poetic wind might also come from the green fields.
It would make us happy, being there.
We would be happy wandering in the endless green countryside.
The poetic wind would blow and blow.
Let Li Po drink and drink wine, and
He would continuously write poems.
We would be in the strong, sweet aroma of Li Po's poetry.
I wish that the world would be filled with fun of poetry.

📖 我喝著月光酒

一杯杯的月光斟滿酒杯裡
這是美好的月光酒
這是故鄉的月
這是故鄉的酒
這是故鄉的月光酒
有故鄉的影子在酒杯裡
舞來舞去
有故鄉的美味在嘴巴裡
嚼來嚼去
故鄉芬芳的花香
飄逸在月光酒裡
給我聞來聞去
使我不忍釋手
永遠抱在身懷裡

📖 I Drink Moonlight Wine

Moonlight fills some wine glasses.
This is wonderful moonlight wine.
This is the moon of my hometown.
This is my hometown wine.
This is the moonlight wine of my hometown.
There is a shadow of my hometown in the wine glass,
Dancing and dancing.
This is a delicacy of my hometown in my mouth.
I chew it and again chew it.
Flowers in my hometown are fragrant.
They are floating in the moonlight wine.
I can smell the fragrance there.
I cannot stop holding it in my hands.
l would always hold it in my arms.

📖 手握時間

時間像鰻魚一樣
很快就溜走
我們要趕快把它抓住
不讓它偷偷游走流失
然而
時間太頑固
我們總是抓不住
無奈的
讓它快速跑走
數十寒暑
飛躍即逝
我們還沒有看完世界美景
還沒有享完世界美食
就悲傷離去

📖 **Seize the Day**

Time is like an eel,
Which is slippery and would run away soon.
We need to hold it quickly and firmly.
Don't let it slip away.
However,
Time is far too stubborn;
We cannot always hold it firmly.
We just cannot help it.
It tends to run away fast.
Dozens of years in my life
Would just pass away quickly.
Regrettably, I have not seen enough the beautiful sceneries of the world,
Nor have I enjoyed enough the world's delicacies.
It is sad that I would leave the world soon.

📖 落葉悲秋

走過嫩葉成長的春天
渡過歡樂的童年
享樂青春美麗的年華
美豔繁花盛開的春夏
被枯黃的秋葉污染
落葉悲傷淚流滿臉
哀傷抓不回失去的春夏時間

📖 Fallen Leaves in Sad Autumn

You have walked through the spring when young leaves grew.
You have been through a happy childhood and
Enjoyed the beautiful years of youth.
You have witnessed beautiful spring and summer, and yet
You are contaminated by withered autumn leaves.
Fallen leaves are sad and tearful which can be seen on their faces.
Sadness cannot recapture the lost spring and summer days.

📖 故鄉的河流唱著歌

我漫步於故鄉的河流
河流唱著我兒時的歌
歡迎我回鄉悠遊
河流流入我的心裡
給我懷鄉甜蜜的溫柔
故鄉的河流喲
你流著,你唱著
唱著我懷鄉之歌
唱著我愛鄉之歌
你是永不枯乾的河流

📖 The River of my Hometown Sings

I walk by the side of the river of my hometown.
The river sings my childhood song
To welcome me home.
The river flows into my mind
Giving me nostalgic sweetness and tenderness.
Oh, the river of my hometown,
Flow on, sing on!
Sing my nostalgic song!
Sing the song of my love for my hometown.
Oh, you are a river that never dries up.

📖 醉人的黃昏

黃昏，昏黃
散發濃濃的酒香
給人沈醉
給人遐想
夕陽的彩霞
散落一地
像灑落滿地的
李白仙詩
給我們醉飲朗誦
充滿無限的樂趣

📖 Twilight that is Intoxicating

It is dusk, and it is twilight.
It is giving off a strong aroma of wine.
It is intoxicating.
It puts me in a reverie.
The glow of the setting sun is
Scattered all over the place
Like outlandish poems by Li Po scattered
Everywhere.
We are intoxicated by recitation of them and
We are having fun.

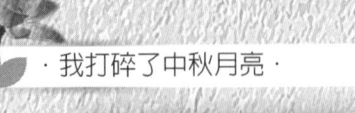

📖 我打碎了中秋月亮

我打碎了中秋月亮
散落一地的金黃月亮
像散落一地的
字字感人的詩篇
那是我的月亮詩、思鄉詩
我夢想著擁抱月亮
深深的懷鄉
和星星月亮共同吟詩歌唱
唱入美麗的夢鄉

📖 I Broke the Mid-Autumn Moon in Pieces

I broke the Mid-Autumn Moon in pieces.
I spread the pieces of the golden moon unto the ground
As if I had scattered
Some touching poems unto the ground.
They were my moon poems, my homesick poems.
I dreamed of hugging the moon
In my deep memory of my hometown.
I would sing along with the stars and the moon and
Sing into a beautiful dream.

📖 莊嚴思索的大山

雄壯的大山
是一個偉大的巨靈
每天莊嚴慎重的思索
思索使地球的生命永存
思索著如何維護這座美麗山水
如何給人類可以快樂的遊山玩水
增進生活樂趣
使萬物生生不息

📖 The Mountain of Solemn Contemplation

The Mountain is majestic.
It is a great giant spirit, which is
Solemn and is engaged in careful thinking every day.
It is thinking how to perpetuate life on the earth,
How to maintain this beautiful landscape and
How human beings can make a happy tour of the mountains and rivers.
The Mountain aims to enhance the joy of life and
To keep things alive.

📖 我每天微笑著生活

這是一個美麗的世界
我要每天微笑著生活
微笑使人生有樂趣
微笑使人生多采多姿
微笑就沒有冰冷的世界
微笑會有火熱的生活
我們要像歡樂奔騰的河流
載著快樂的魚群
到處遊戲
四處樂游
快樂跳舞
快樂唱歌
過著美好的生活

📖 I Live with Smiles Every Day

It is a beautiful world.
I want to live with smiles every day.
Smiles make life fun.
Smiles make life colorful.
Without smiles, the world would be a cold place.
Smiles would make life hot.
What we need is a river of joy, which
Would carry happy fish.
They would play games everywhere.
They would get around happily,
Dance happily and
Sing songs happily.
All they have to do is to live a good life.

📖 天上的星星是我們的眼睛

天上的星星是我們的眼睛
他們可以看見世間的萬事萬物
可以看見人類的善行和惡行
全都會報告給天神
積善之家有餘慶
這是天神賜給我們的恩情
我們只要天天有善行
星星才會很高興
一閃一閃亮晶晶
像電訊報給天神
就會保佑我們

📖 The Stars in the Sky are our Eyes

The stars in the sky are our eyes.
They can see everything in the world.
They can tell the good from the bad of human beings.
They would report them to the gods in heaven.
The family that does good all the time would be blessed.
This is grace that the gods would give us.
As long as we do good every day,
The stars would be happy:
Twinkle, Twinkle, Little Star.
Their twinkling is like the telegraph sending messages to the gods.
They would bless us.

📖 還你一湖水

當我口渴時
你給我了一杯水
我很感謝你
我會還你一湖水
當我飢餓時
你給我一碗飯
我很感謝你
我會還你一糧倉的米
我們的心臟,雖只有拳頭大
但是我們感恩的心比海洋還大
海洋可以潤澤飢渴的人類
海洋可以潤澤乾旱的地球
給我們滿載豐收
我們有感恩的心
就會有天大的福報和歡欣

📖 I Shall Return a Lake of Water to You

When I am thirsty,
You give me a glass of water.
I am very grateful to you.
I shall give you back a lake of water.
When I am hungry,
You give me a bowl of rice.
I am very grateful to you.
I shall return a granary of rice to you.
Even though our heart is as small as a fist,
Yet our gratitude is bigger than the ocean.
The ocean could help quench the thirst of humans.
The ocean could also moisten a parched earth, which
Would give us a full harvest.
Being grateful,
We would be greatly granted with joy and blessings.

喝了美酒的夕陽

喝了美酒的夕陽
滿臉通紅
不慎跌落海底
讓我們婉惜
無限好的夕陽
只給我們片刻的歡喜
一寸光陰,一寸金
一輪夕陽,一份美意
我們要好好珍惜
永不分離
我們擁抱著溫暖的夕陽
蓋著天上漂亮的彩雲棉被
呼呼大睡
睡到天亮
和太陽共同起床
又迎接了新的一天美好時光

📖 The Sun at Dusk Seemed to Have Been Drunk

The sun at dusk seemed to have been drunk,
Blushed all over.
It accidentally fell to the bottom of the sea,
For which we felt regretful.
The beauty of sunset was infinite
Which gave us only a moment of joy.
An inch of time is worth more than an inch of gold.
A sunset gives beauty.
We should cherish it.
We should never be separate from it.
Embracing the warm sunset and
Covered with a quilt of the beautiful colorful clouds in the sky,
We would sleep soundly
Till dawn.
We would wake up with the sun to
Welcome another beautiful day.

📖 每一朵花都有存在的理由

每一朵花都有存在的理由
每一個人都有存在的理由
每一首詩都有存在的理由
每一朵花,都努力成為最美麗的花
不管風吹雨打,都要成長
開出最美麗的花
每一個人都有存在的理由
都要努力的成長
成為英雄,聖賢
每一首詩都有存在的理由
詩含自我存在的詩意
和感動人心的存在價值

📖 Every Flower Has a Reason to Exist

Every flower has a reason to exist.
Everyone has a reason to exist.
Every poem has a reason to exist.
Every flower strives to grow as a most beautiful flower.
Rain or shine, the flower would grow
To be a most beautiful one.
Everyone has a reason to exist.
One has to grow hard
To be a hero or a sage.
Every poem has a reason to exist.
Poetry contains the elements of self-existence—
The value of touching its readers.

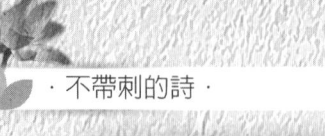

📖 不帶刺的詩

　　玫瑰帶刺最美
　　完美的詩,不帶刺最美麗
　　完美的詩有芬芳的花香
　　完美的詩有可口的甜湯
　　完美的詩有優美的歌唱
　　完美的詩不要刺
　　也勝過萬朵玫瑰花
　　勝過萬朵牡丹花
　　勝過滿園盛開的花

📖 Poetry without Thorns

Roses with thorns are the most beautiful.
Perfect poetry is beautiful, but it has no thorns.
Perfect poetry has a fragrant floral flavor.
Perfect poetry is like delicious, sweet soup.
Reading perfect poetry is like singing beautiful songs.
Perfect poetry does not need thorns.
It is better than ten thousand roses,
Ten thousand peonies or
A garden of blooming flowers.

📖 寫在河流的詩

把我們的詩，寫在河流上
這些詩，富含鄉土味
充滿生命力
深藏詩韻味
充分表現純詩的意境和真諦
河流上的詩
會流到汨羅江
和屈原相會
和楚辭相映輝煌
給世人永久欣賞

📖 Poems Written on the River

Let us write our poems on the river.
They would be rich in local flavor and
Full of life force.
They would be profound in meaning.
They would carry the artistic conception of pure poetry.
On the river,
They would converge with River Miluo and
Meet Qu Yuan.
Together with Chuci,
They would be there for the world to enjoy forever.

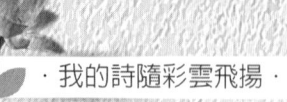

📖 我的詩隨彩雲飛揚

我的詩隨彩雲飛揚
飛到高高的天上
飛到太陽邊
成為熱情澎湃的詩
飛到月亮邊
成為嬌美少女的情詩
飛到星星邊
成為一群快樂跳舞的兒童詩
我的詩隨彩雲飛揚
四處漂泊流浪
像李白那樣
心胸坦蕩蕩
飛到天上摘星
和彩雲一起飛揚

📖 I Wish that my Poems Would Fly with the Colorful Clouds

I wish that my poems would fly with the colorful clouds.
They would be high in the sky.
Flying to the sun,
They would be poems about passionate love.
Flying to the moon,
They would be beautiful girls' love poems.
Flying to the stars,
They would be poems for and about a group of happily dancing children.
I wish that my poems would fly with the colorful clouds.
They would be wandering around
Like Li Po's poems.
Open-minded,
Li Po seems to have flown to the stars in the sky,
Dancing with the colorful clouds.

📖 讓我們的憂愁交給河流

不管是水流悠悠
還是波濤洶湧
都能載走我們的憂愁
不管是幾毫克的憂愁
還是千斤重的的憂愁
都會被河流載走
流入大海
變成海浪
歡樂跳舞
消除千愁

📖 Let us Hand our Sorrows over to the River

Whether the water is flowing leisurely or
It is roaring and choppy,
The river could take away our sorrows.
Whether it is a few milligrams of sadness or
Thousands of tons of sadness,
The river water could carry it away.
The river water would flow into the sea and
Become sea waves.
The sea waves would dance with joy and
Take away thousands of sorrows of ours.

📖 花美花香花悅耳

花美花香花悅耳
花是人類最良好的朋友
我們到花園散步
欣賞花的美艷
聞聞花的芳香
聽聽花的樂音
享受花的盛宴
勝過山珍海味的大餐

📖 Flowers are Beautiful, Fragrant and Melodious

Flowers are beautiful, fragrant and melodious.

They are our best friends.

Let's take a walk in the garden.

We shall admire the beauty of flowers,

Smell the sweetness of flowers, and

Listen to the music of flowers.

We shall enjoy a feast of flowers,

Which would surpass the delicacies of a sumptuous banquet.

詩歌插在雲雀的翅膀

詩歌 在雲雀的翅膀
文字也會飛翔
我們的詩歌
就由東方唱到西方
由南方唱到北方
由鄉村唱到城市
由原野唱到山林
由海上唱到天上
成為歡樂的詩歌世界
和美妙的天堂

📖 If We Inserted Poetry on a Lark's Wings

If we inserted poetry on a lark's wings,
Words would also fly.
Our poetry
Would sing from east to west,
From south to north,
From the country to the city,
From the wilderness to the forest, and
From the sea to the sky.
The world would be joyful and be one of poetry.
It would be a wonderful paradise.

📖 美麗芬芳的花朵擁抱陽光

一大片原野的美麗芬芳的花朵
熱情的擁抱陽光
讓陽光更加芳香
讓世界更美麗芳香
這是一個美麗的新世界
是上帝賜給我們的歡樂世界
這是我們的天堂
我們永遠存在的天堂

📖 Beautiful, Fragrant Flowers are Embracing the Sun

A large field of beautiful, fragrant flowers are
Warmly embracing the sun,
Making the sun more fragrant and
The world more beautiful and fragrant.
This is a brave new world.
This is a joyful world God has sent us.
This is our paradise.
This is our heaven which would exist forever.

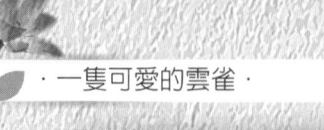

一隻可愛的雲雀

一隻可愛的雲雀
飛姿美妙
它飛過的彩影
是一幅美麗的圖畫
它飛過的歌聲
是寫在空中的美妙詩歌
它是我們親密的文友
也是親密的藝友
它多才多藝
給我們的世界多采多姿

📖 A Cute Lark

A cute lark there is,
Flying beautifully.
The shadow it flew over
Is a beautiful picture.
The melody it flew through
Is a beautiful poem written in the air.
The lark is our close friend in the arts
And in literature.
The lark is versatile, and
Is able to make our world colorful.

把我們的詩交給鳥兒歌唱

我們寫的詩
不管是古典詩,還是現代詩
不管是老人詩,還是兒童詩
不管是鄉土詩,還是海洋詩
不管是愛情詩,還是親情詩
都要交給鳥兒歌唱
可以在原野歌唱
可以在森林歌唱
可以在家裡歌唱
可以在學校歌唱

📖 Let us Give our Poems to the Birds to Sing

Whether the poems we write
Are classical or modernist,
Are for old men, or for children,
Are about the native or about the maritime,
Are about love affairs or the family,
Let us give them to the birds to sing.
They will sing them in the wilderness,
In the forest,
In the home and
In the school.

📖 不要吹熄別人的燈火

有燈大家點
有燈大家亮
讓世界光明
讓宇宙光亮
把別人的燈熄滅變黑暗
不會使你更光明
當別人的燈火將熄滅時
我們更要給它再點亮
讓世界永續光芒

📖 Don't Blow out Other People's Lights

There are lights for all.
There are lights for everyone.
All the lights would make the world bright.
All the lights would also make the universe radiant.
Your putting out other people's lights
Would not make you brighter.
When someone else's lights go out,
We should help rekindle them
To continue to make the world shine out.

📖 我是一隻雲雀

我是一隻雲雀
歌聲嘹亮
由東方唱到西方
歌聲中有我的詩詞
這是一首優美的歌曲
由東方唱到西方
由南方唱到北方
唱響宇宙四方
讓我們聽得無限快樂舒暢

📖 I Wish I were a Lark

I wish I were a lark.
I would sing loudly.
I would sing from east to west.
There would be poetry in my song.
It is a beautiful song,
Ringing from east to west and
From south to north.
My song would be resounding through the universe.
Those who have heard my song would be infinitely joyful and comfortable.

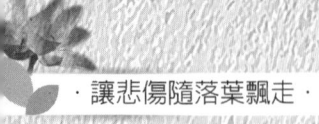

📖 讓悲傷隨落葉飄走

微笑是給生長新葉的祝福
歡樂是給盛開花朵盛宴
盛開的花朵,永遠歡樂
不要悲傷
讓悲傷隨落葉飄走
給我們心境平和
沒有憂愁
只有幸福快樂

📖 Let Sadness Drift Away with Fallen Leaves

A smile is given as a blessing for growing new leaves.
Joy is a feast because of blooming flowers.
Blooming flowers always bring happiness.
We should not be sad.
Let our sadness drift away with fallen leaves.
What we need is peace of mind.
There would not be worries.
There would only be happiness.

📖 把生活變成詩

生活很苦
生活很悶
我要把生活變成詩
變成快樂的詩
變成美麗的詩
生活才有意義
詩是人類的救命符
有了詩，人生才有意義
有了詩，人生才會快樂幸福

📖 Let us Turn Life into Poetry

Life is hard;
Life is boring.
I would turn life into a poem.
It would be a happy poem.
It would be a beautiful poem.
Then, life would make sense.
Poetry should be a lifesaver of mankind.
With poetry, life would be full of meaning;
With poetry, there would be bliss and happiness in life.

📖 把自己當鑽石磨亮

鑽石要琢磨才會晶亮
愈磨愈亮
我們的學問愈學愈深愈廣
我們人品愈修愈高尚
我們的武藝愈練愈高強
我門的技藝愈磨愈成熟
我們要日夜磨亮
愈磨愈亮
永遠光亮

📖 Polish Yourself like a Diamond

Diamonds need to be polished to shine.
The more you polish, the brighter the diamond would be.
The more you study, the deeper and wider your knowledge would be.
The more you cultivate, the more noble your character would be.
The more you practice, the better your martial arts would be.
The more you hone, the more mature your skills would be.
You have to polish and practice day and night
To get a better and brighter future.
If you do so, the way ahead you would be bright.

📖 相逢是首詩

太陽和海洋相逢是首詩
是燦爛輝煌的詩
月亮和星星相逢是首詩
是優美感人的詩
父母兄弟姐妹相逢是首詩
是天倫歡樂的詩
情人相逢是首詩
是纏綿不斷的詩
都是有緣來相逢
相逢使我們不再孤獨
相逢給我們歡樂無比
和樂融融

📖 Meeting is a Poem

The meeting of the sun and the ocean is a poem;
It is a brilliant poem.
The meeting of the moon and the stars is a poem;
It is a beautiful and touching poem.
The meeting of parents, brothers and sisters is a poem;
It is a happy poem.
The meeting of lovers is a poem;
It is a passionate poem.
Some are predestined to meet others.
Meeting makes us no longer alone and lonely.
Meeting makes us joyful and
Happy.

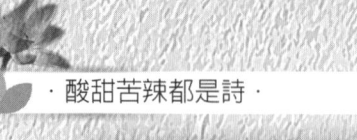

📖 酸甜苦辣都是詩

人生有酸甜苦辣
就像有起伏的海浪
也有山峰和低谷
也有雨天和豔陽
酸甜苦辣都是詩
悲傷和快樂也是詩
我們要抓住快樂的詩
忘記悲傷的詩
並忘記酸甜苦辣的詩
我們要留著甜蜜的詩
讓世界都快樂甜蜜

📖 Ups and Downs in Life Could be Poetry

There are ups and downs in life, which is
Like rolling waves.
There are mountain peaks and valleys;
There are rainy days and sunny days.
Ups and downs in life could be poetry.
Poetry could be about sadness and happiness.
We have to grasp firmly the happy poetry and
Forget about sadness in poetry.
Let us forget about the poetry of ups and downs and
Keep sweet poetry.
What we need is to make the world sweet and happy.

微笑是最美麗的語言

微笑是最美麗的語言
微笑是最美麗的圖畫
微笑是最美麗的音樂
微笑是最美麗的詩篇
希望每天都有微笑和陽光
使人生燦爛
微笑使我們登入幸福快樂的天堂

📖 Smile is the Most Beautiful Language

Smile is the most beautiful language.
Smile is the most beautiful picture.
Smile is the most beautiful music.
Smile is the most beautiful poetry.
I hope there will be smiles and sunshine every day,
Which will make life bright.
A smile brings us to a happy paradise.

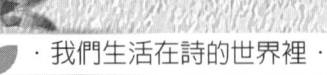

📖 我們生活在詩的世界裡

這是一個詩的世界
我們生活在詩的世界裡
詩是舒適的人間溫床
詩裡有微笑的春陽
對著微笑的星星和月亮
聞聞充滿詩意芬芳的花香
我們生活在詩的世界裡
全身沾滿詩意
煥發著詩的光芒

📖 We Live in a World of Poetry

This is a world of poetry.
We live in a world of poetry.
Poetry is a comfortable hotbed.
There is a smiling spring sun in the poem,
Smiling at the stars and the moon.
Let us smell the poetic fragrance of flowers and
We shall live in a world of poetry.
We would be full of poetry and
Glow with poetry.

📖 花好月圓

我們希望——
有美好的宇宙
有美好的世界
天天花好月圓
沒有花凋花落
沒有月缺月失
只有永遠的花好月圓
快樂億萬年

📖 A Full Moon and Good Flowers

We wish that--
There would be a beautiful universe and
A beautiful world.
There would be flowers every day.
No flowers would wither and go away.
The moon would be full all the time.
Flowers would be perpetually in full blossom and the moon would be perpetually full.

📖 像月亮一樣的愛

父母的愛像月亮的光芒
獻給全世界的子女
感恩難忘
嚴父之情,慈母之愛
愛像月亮的光芒
閃耀萬丈
月亮照耀我們的身體
月亮照耀我們的心靈
給我們無限舒暢
月亮像一座明燈
指引我們前行
讓我們不會迷失
讓我們充滿愛意
生活愜意
充滿和氣
讓世界美麗

📖 Parents' Love is like the Light of the Moon

Parents' love is like the light of the moon.
Their love is dedicated to the children of the world.
We should be thankful to them, and we should not forget them.
Strict as a father and loving as a mother,
Their love is like the light of the moon,
Shining over the earth.
The moon shines on our bodies.
The moon shines on our hearts.
It gives us infinite comfort.
The moon, which is like a beacon,
Would guide us on our way to the future
So that we wouldn't get lost.
The moon would fill us with love, and
Lead us to live a comfortable life.
There would be peace and
Beauty in our world.

📖 我打碎了夕陽

為了留住夕陽上
最大，最美麗的彩霞
我打碎了夕陽
不讓整個夕陽
落入海底
落入黑暗
落入虛無
變成永不落西山的太陽
像切後再生的肝臟
變成漂亮的夕陽
我將再生圓圓的夕陽
高掛在玉山上
成為台灣的希望
和台灣的光芒

📖 I Wish to Break Down the Sunset into Pieces

To keep the biggest and most beautiful rainbow on
The sunset,
I wish to break down the sunset into pieces.
I would not let the whole sunset
fall into the bottom of the sea,
Or into darkness,
Or into nothingness.
I wish that the sun would never set,
Like a regenerated human liver.
It would become a perpetually beautiful sunset.
I would like to hang the regenerated round sunset
High on Mount Jade.
It would be hope and
Light to the island of Taiwan.

📖 雲是天上的飛鳥

一朵朵天上的白雲
一朵朵天邊的彩雲
飛在天上
像一群群飛鳥
在天上翱翔
無憂無慮
一起自由飛翔
在空中跳舞，歡樂歌唱
給我們快樂的遐想
渾身舒暢

📖 Clouds are Birds in the Sky

White clouds in the sky and
Colorful clouds at the west side of the sky
All fly there
like a flock of birds
Soaring in the sky
Care-freely.
They fly freely together
Dancing in the air and singing with joy.
They give us happy reveries and
Make us feel comfortable.

📖 星星是天上的明珠

星星是天上的明珠
閃閃爍爍
有千萬個億萬個
我們都是摘星的人
左手摘一個
右手摘一個
全人類摘了一百五十億個
裝滿了地球
使地球亮麗
使人人富有
　人人快樂

📖 Stars Are Pearls in the Sky

Stars are pearls in the sky,
Twinkling.
There are billions upon billions of them there.
If we were all catchers of stars.
We could catch one with our right hand and another in our left one.
If all souls on the earth could catch them this way,
The earth would be filled with fifteen billion stars.
Our world would be gorgeous.
Each and every one of us would be rich and
Happy.

📖 明天的天空會更蔚藍

不要怕今天的陰雨
不要怕今天的狂風暴雨
我們期待可愛的明天
我們期待晴空萬里的明天
明天的太陽會升起
趕走陰雨和暴雨
使天空更亮麗
明天的天空會更蔚藍如碧玉
它會消除我們心裡的悲傷和憂鬱
使我們快樂歡喜

📖 I Wish that the Sky Tomorrow Would be Bluer

Don't be scared by today's rain.
Don't be scared by today's storms and rain showers.
We wish that it would be better and more lovable tomorrow and
That there would be clear skies tomorrow.
The sun tomorrow would rise and
Dispel storms and rain showers.
The sky would be more gorgeous.
The sky would be as blue as a sapphire.
The blue sky would drive away sadness and melancholy.
We would then be happy and blissful.

📖 月亮為你歌唱

星星為你跳舞
月亮為你歌唱
太陽給你光明和能量
我愛星星,月亮和太陽
因為他們是我們的父母
兄弟,姊妹和朋友
大家一起快樂生活
使地球成為歡樂的天堂

📖 I Wish that the Moon Would Sing for You

I wish that the stars would dance for you and
That the moon would sing for you.
The sun gives you light and energy.
I love the sun, the moon and the stars
Because they are like my parents, and siblings and friends.
Together, we would live happily, and
All in the world would live happily as in a paradise.

📖 雲給月亮蓋上了棉被

雲是月亮的親密情人
月亮高掛在天上
高處不勝寒
有親密的情人―雲
守護在月亮身邊
並給月亮蓋上軟軟的棉被
使她舒服溫暖
月亮是最幸福的快樂女神

📖 The Cloud Covers the Moon with a Quilt

The cloud is the moon's beloved.
The moon is high in the sky.
It is cold there.
The cloud, the moon's loving sweetheart, is
Standing by to guard her and
Covering her with a soft quilt.
The moon is warm and is
The most blessed and happiest goddess.

📖 像美酒的詩獻給月亮

月亮太美
月亮太可愛
我把像美酒的詩
獻給月亮姑娘
她喝得醉醺醺
載歌載舞在天上
溫柔的月亮
照耀我們的地球
給我們快樂
大家共同跳舞歌唱

📖 I Wish to Dedicate Wine-like Poetry to the Moon

The moon is beautiful.
The moon is lovable.
I wish to dedicate my wine-like poetry
To the moon, the beautiful young lady.
She would be so intoxicated
That she would dance and sing in the sky.
Her light is soft and is
Beaming at us, which
Makes us happy.
Let us all dance and sing with her.

家是天堂

不管颱風下雨
家是我們的避風港
家是我們的天堂

家有我兒時的記憶
家有父母的汗滴
家有祖父母的陳年老酒
也有古老的傢俱

溫柔的月光
含情脈脈,穿越白雲和藍天
照在我的臉龐和頭上
照耀我的故鄉

月亮像熱情的歸雁
銜著電燈和家書
飛回我的家鄉

📖 The Home is Like Paradise

Rain or shine,
The home is our haven.
The home is our paradise.

The home contains the recollections of our childhood,
Our parents' sweat drops,
Old collections of wine by our grandparents and
Antique furniture.

Affectionately,
   the moon flying over the white clouds in the blue sky,
Beaming with her light on my face and my head and
My hometown.

Moonlight is like passionate returning wild geese
Carrying electric light and letters
To my hometown,

・家是天堂・

照耀我的家鄉
那是我的天堂
我要像一隻飛雁
飛回我的家
飛回我的天堂

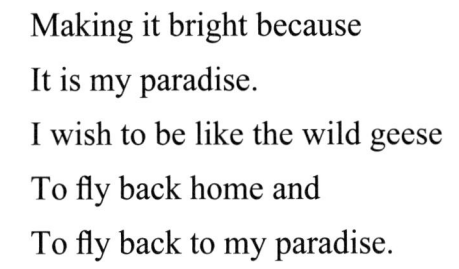

· The Home is Like Paradise ·

Making it bright because
It is my paradise.
I wish to be like the wild geese
To fly back home and
To fly back to my paradise.

憂鬱的月亮

男女哀哀怨怨
愛的不被愛
不被愛的又愛人
愛了以後又分離
月亮看了很憂傷
希望牽紅線成婚
將憂傷消失於無形

遊子漂流四方
常常思鄉
淚流滿臉悲傷
月亮看了也憂傷
希望用一絲絲一線線的月光
牽引遊子回鄉
和月亮共聚
歡樂一堂

📖 **The Sad Moon**

Lovers are sad and sorrowful because
The one who loves would not be loved by the other, and
The one who is not loved would love the other.
Those in love would separate.
Knowing this, the moon becomes sad and is
Trying to make amends.
The moon would help drive away their sadness and sorrow.

Wanderers in all directions
In alien places are
Homesick and
Sad and tearful.
Knowing this, the moon also becomes sad.
She wishes to use her slight light
To guide them home.
She wishes to be together with the wanderers.

📖 有翅膀的夢想

我們的夢想
都長著翅膀
可以飛到東飛到西
到處遊戲
飛到高高的天上
展現高昂的志氣
可以飛到花園
吸取甜蜜的花蜜
四處觀賞花朵的美麗
也可飛到情人床邊
訴說綿綿的愛意
永不分離

📖 Dreams with Wings

Our dreams
All have wings.
They can fly east and west
To play everywhere.
They can fly high into the sky
To show their high ambitions.
They can fly to the garden
To suck the sweet nectar from the flowers.
They can see the beauty of flowers everywhere.
They can also fly to their beloved's bedsides
To tell their love to their beloved and
They would never separate.

妳是人間最美的情歌

妳是人間最美的情歌
可以感動宇宙的心房
可以感動億萬人的心臟
妳是歌舞中的天仙玉女
歌聲更優美嘹亮
舞姿曼妙
越舞越漂亮
給人無限讚賞

📖 You are the Most Beautiful Love Song in the World

You are the most beautiful love song in the world.
You can touch the heart of the universe.
You can touch the hearts of millions of people.
You are the fairy goddess in singing and dancing.
Your singing is more beautiful and louder than anything else.
You can dance gracefully.
The more you dance, the more beautiful you are,
Earning infinite admiration from us.

📖 我們的愛情堅若鑽石

我們的愛情堅若鑽石
不是一盤散沙
清風一吹就飛走，遠離
我們的愛情堅若鑽石
不能切割
不能分離
堅硬無比
永遠緊密的結合在一起

📖 Our Love Is as Firm as a Diamond

Our love is as firm as a diamond.
It is not a mess of sand
Which would be blown far away even by a breeze.
Our love is as firm as a diamond which
Cannot be cut and
Separated.
It would remain extremely solid.
We shall always be closely combined together.

📖 傾斜的郵筒

綠色的郵筒
你裝載了太多情書和憂傷
你裝載了太多眼淚和愁悵
一陣颱風
吹彎了你沉重的脊梁
令人哀傷

📖 A Slanted Postbox

The green postbox,
You have been loaded with too many love letters and sadness.
You have been loaded with too many tears and worries.
A typhoon came and
Bent your heavy spine.
We are sad about your disfiguration.

叩頭須要叩到泥土裡

叩頭不只要彎腰九十度
更要叩到泥土裡
叩到泥土裡
才會生根，開花，結果

我愛妳
不只愛入骨髓
更愛入泥土裡
這才是真心的愛意
永不分離

我愛真理
也要愛入泥土裡
才能開出真理之花
結出真理果實
悟出人生的意義

📖 If One Kowtows, One Has to Do So as to Touch the Dirt

To kowtow is not just bending oneself over ninety degrees.
One has to do it so much as to hit the dirt.
Doing so, it would amount to knocking into the dirt,
Which would help take roots, blossom, bear fruit.

In the same manner, I love you.
I would love you deeply as into the bone marrow of mine.
I would also do so as if deeply into the dirt.
I would think this is true love.
Then, we would never separate.

Again, in the same manner, I love truth.
I would love it so deeply as into the dirt
So much so as to grow the flower of truth and
Bear fruit of truth.
I would then fully understand the meaning of life.

📖 用愛畫妳

我用愛畫妳
畫成可愛的百靈鳥
放在我的心裡
放在我的胸懷裡
天天唱著情歌
快樂無比

我用愛畫妳
畫成小巧玲瓏的維納斯
放在我的心裡
放在我的胸懷裡
搔首弄姿
媚來眼去
給我溫暖舒適
給我樂趣
永遠相愛
永不分離

📖 Drawing a Picture of You with Love

I would like to draw a picture of you with love.
I would like to draw a picture of you as a cute lark and
Put it in my heart,
In my chest.
There you would
Happily sing love songs every day.

I would like to draw a picture of you with love.
I would like to draw a picture of you as a small and exquisite Venus and
Put it in my heart,
In my chest.
There, you would scratch
And wink,
Giving me warmth and comfort
And joy.
We shall love each other and
Would never separate.

📖 我是高山

我是高山
比喜馬拉雅山還高
巍巍然,高聳入天
在天上和星星月亮太陽做遊戲
談情說愛
談詩
談地球和太空的秘密
給我們智慧和禪意

📖 I Wish that I Were a High Mountain

I wish that I were a high mountain,
Higher than the Himalayas,
So towering that I would reach the sky.
I would play games with stars, moon and sun in the sky.
There, I would fall in love with them all.
We would talk about poetry and
The secrets of earth and space.
Then, I would gain wisdom and Chan Buddhism therefrom.

📖 愛是一條河

愛是一條河
愛是一條甜蜜的河
愛是永不枯乾的河流
日日夜夜流
愛是世界上最偉大的河
可以沖洗世間的污穢
可以解除我們的憂愁
使我們永遠快樂

📖 Love is like a River

Love is like a river.
It is a sweet river which
Will never dry up.
It flows day and night.
Love is the greatest river in the world which
Can wash away the filth of the world and
Relieve us of worries,
Making us happy forever.

📖 多情的花

花是人類的情人
阿娜多姿,笑臉迎人
世間有那麼多花朵
人人有愛
花花有情
七十五億人類
有七十五億花朵
投入我們的懷抱
任我們擁吻
吐露芳香
展現美麗
展演秀氣
給世界帶來歡樂的氣息

📖 Amorous Flowers

Flowers are the lovers of mankind.
They are pretty, colorful and smiling.
With so many flowers in the world,
I wish that people would be in love.
Flowers are lovely.
There are seven and a half billion humans in the world, and
There should be seven and a half billion flowers
In the arms of each of us.
Let us kiss the flowers.
Let them give off fragrance,
Show their beauty and
Exhibit their graceful figures.
I believe that they would bring joy to the world.

月餅

月餅是地球上不會發光的月亮
一到中秋節就擺滿街上
許多地球上的月亮被吃掉了
只有天上光明的月亮沒被吃掉
否則明年中秋節就沒月亮可看

📖 **Mooncakes**

On earth, mooncakes are moons that do not glow.

At Mid-autumn Festival, they are everywhere to be found in the market.

Many of the earthly moons are eaten.

I wish that the one in the sky would not be eaten;

Otherwise, there would be no moon for us to see next Mid-autumn Festival.

📖 一朵美麗的花

一朵美麗的花
很乖很可愛
她乖乖地站在花枝上
向人微笑
請你們不要欺侮她
請你們不要採擷她
留給大家欣賞

📖 A Beautiful Flower

A beautiful flower,
Quietly and lovably,
Grows on a twig of a tree.
She is smiling at passers-by.
Please don't bully her.
Please don't destroy her.
She is there for everyone to enjoy her beauty.

📖 初秋的落葉

一片最有情的樹葉
聞到秋天的氣息
就悲傷起來
不小心從樹上掉落下來
離別了他的父母兄弟姊妹
流浪在泥土上
嗦嗦地哭訴流浪的痛苦

📖 Fallen Leaves in Early Autumn

A sentimental leaf,
Smelling the breath of the coming autumn,
Is sad.
He accidentally falls down from the tree,
Leaving his parents, brothers and sisters.
He wanders everywhere on earth,
Tremblingly crying and telling the pains of his wandering life.

📖 花兒笑什麼

花兒高興的笑著
向蜜蜂說
請你們盡量來吻我，擁抱我
讓我們共同合唱愛情交響曲
讓世界充滿愛情
　　　充滿和平
花兒高興的向我們微笑
要大家像蜜蜂一樣擁吻我
共譜結婚進行曲

花兒向我們微笑
願七十五億人，像七十五億花朵
讓七十五億隻蜜蜂來擁吻
共同和樂
共同歡欣

📖 Why Is the Flower Smiling

The flower smiles happily and
Says to the bees,
"Please kiss me and hug me as much as you can.
Let's sing the symphony of love together and
Fill the world with love and
      With peace."
The flower smiles happily at us and
Wants everyone to kiss me like a bee and to
Sing the wedding march together.

The flower smiles at us.
May the 7.5 billion people be like 7.5 billion flowers
Kissed by the 7.5 billion bees.
I wish that there would be common harmony and
Happiness together.

📖 像雨一樣的淚水

風呼呼的吹
像雨一樣的淚水
嘩啦,嘩啦
一直流著,一直流著
唯恐魔鬼要破壞台灣
要把淡水河吸乾
要把愛河吸乾
抽空台灣

使善良的台灣人民
哀哀怨怨
像雨一樣,淚流滿面
流著,流著
注滿淡水河和愛河
讓台灣的生命力鮮活

📖 Tears Drop like Rain Showers

Wind is howling, and
Tears are dropping like rain showers.
Whoa, whoa!
Tears keep bursting and bursting out
Because the Evil One is destroying Taiwan.
She is draining water out of River Danshui in Taipei and
Water out of River Love in Kaohsiung.
She is hollowing out the resources of Taiwan.

What she has been doing makes the kind-hearted people of Taiwan
Sad and grievous.
The people of Taiwan are weeping with tears streaming all over their faces.
Their tears are flowing and flowing.
I wish that the tears would fill up River Dansui and River Love.
I wish that the life of Taiwan would be full of vitality.

台灣美酒灌醉了太陽

我坐在玉山上
舉杯台灣美酒
灌醉了太陽
滿臉紅光
我們乞求祂給我們光明美麗
　　　　　　　　繁榮富裕
並給我們快樂健康
永久和平安詳

📖 Let the Sun Get Drunk with Taiwan' Wine

Sitting on the summit of Mount Jade,
I proposed a toast of Taiwan's wine
To the sun and get him drunk.
The sun was blushing.
We would pray that he give us light and beauty,
                    Affluence and prosperity.
We wish that he would give us happiness, health,
And perpetual peace as well.

📖 喝醉的雨

喝醉的雨
把李白灌醉了
寫出不朽的詩

喝醉的雨
把楚民灌醉了
眾人皆醉,皆濁
唯獨屈原不醉,清醒

二十一世紀的現代人
被喝醉的雨灌飽後
昏昏沈沈
喜歡吵架,戰爭
我們要請佛陀和上帝來解酒
讓人類清醒,和平

📖 The Rain that Has Been Drunk

The rain that had been drunk
Got Li Po (701–762) so drunk that
He could have written some immortal poems.

However, the rain that had been drunk
Got the Chu people drunk as well.
Everybody was drunk and the world was filthy.
Only Qu Yuan (c. 340 BC–278 BC) was sober and not drunk.

People in the twenty-first century
Are so drunk because of the drunk rain
That they seem to be sleepy all the time.
In their sleep, they tend to fight and to make wars,
Needing the Buddha and Jesus
To wake them up. Then, there would be peace in the world.

📖 綿綿情歌飛翔雲間

綿綿情歌飛翔雲間
青春活力充滿人間
這是愛的世界
這是情的世界
這是可愛的世界
白雲回送給我們歡樂
白雲賜給我們永浴愛河

📖 Love Songs Flying in the Clouds

Love songs are flying in the clouds.
They make the world youthful and vigorous.
This is a world of love.
This is a world of passion.
This is a lovely world.
The white clouds send joy back to us.
The white clouds give us eternal love.

📖 愛是最美的風景

我們不必坐車,
坐飛機
到世界的名勝古蹟觀光旅遊

只要有愛
不管你住茅屋或豪宅
都能擁有最美的風景
像於萬花齊放的花園散步
享受人生最大樂趣

📖 Love Is the Most Beautiful Scenic Spot

Only if there is love,
We don't have to travel, by car or by plane, far
To visit any historic spot.

Only if there is love,
    whether we live in a humble cottage or a huge mansion,
We would walk in a garden where flowers are blooming
And enjoy the greatest bliss in our life.

📖 我是天上的雲朵

我是天上的雲朵
天上的雲朵都是我的好朋友
使我不寂寞
我跟那些雲朵
飛來飛去
一起遊戲
非常快樂

📖 If I Were a Cloud in the Sky

If I were a cloud in the sky.
I would be friends with all the others.
I would not be lonely.
I would play with them.
Flying here and there.
Playing together,
We would be happy.

📖 海的大肚量

海有大肚量
可以吞食大魚、小魚
可以吞食大船、小船
可以吞食萬里奔騰的疲憊大江、小河
可以吞食情人的歡笑和眼淚
可以消除你的喜怒和悲傷
看了大海的層層波濤駭浪
會增強我們的生命力量
讓我們歡樂歌唱

📖 The Sea Has a Huge Capacity

The sea has a huge capacity.
She takes fish, big and small.
She takes boats, big and small.
She receives rivers that have flowed tirelessly from faraway places.
She even takes lover's tears and laughters.
The sea may confort us in our sadness and happiness.
Watching her waves rolling over to us,
We would be full of energy of life.
We would be able to receive, like the sea, rivers that have flowed
    from long distances and
We would even take lover's tears and laughters.
We would rid ourselves of anger and sadness.
Watching her waves rolling over to us,
We would be full of energy of life, nd
We would be singing songs happily.

📖 白雲飄著我的詩想

白雲飄在藍藍的天上
白雲飄著我的詩想
我的詩寫在白雲間
寫給天公看
寫給人類看
讓天空和人間充滿詩想
讓宇宙充滿美妙的詩篇

📖 The White Cluods Are Carrying My Poetry

Floating high in the azure sky,
The white clouds are carrying my poetry.
Written in between the clouds,
My poetry is for Grandpa Heaven to read
And for the people to read.
I wish that there would be poetry in heaven and on earth
And that the universe would be filled with my wonderful poetry.

📖 天上有很多星星是我們的眼睛

天上有很多星星
是我們的眼睛
它們在探索太空的秘密
它們也傳達很多情人的愛情
訴說許多甜言蜜語
給我們歡樂的情趣
和幸福的喜氣

📖 I Wish that the Many Stars in the Sky Would Be Our Eyes

There are many stars in the sky.
I wish that they would be our eyes.
With them, we would explore the secret of the outer space.
They would also spread the love and
Sweet messages between the two beloved everywhere,
Giving happiness and
Bliss to all.

📖 海是我的愛人

藍色的海
溫柔體貼
她是我親密的愛人
她會洗淨我人生的煩惱
她任我撫摸
　　任我擁抱
她是我親密的愛人

📖 The Sea Is My Sweetheart

The azure sea is
Tender and considerate.
She is my sweetheart.
She helps cleanse my worries.
She lets me touch her and
She lets me embrace her.
She is my sweetheart.

📖 上弦月之吻

上弦月以溫柔的櫻唇吻我
我以熱情的心回吻她
可以吻出妳自然的芳香
連我寫給妳的詩也芳香

📖 A Kiss from the First Quarter Moon

The first quarter moon caresses and kisses me with her cherry lips, and
I kiss her back passionately.
I can smell her natural fragrance, and
The poem I wrote for her is as fragrant.

📖 七夕情歌

七夕情歌瀰漫天邊
七夕情歌響徹藍天
天長地久的愛情
一直綿延
一直綿延

📖 Love Songs on te Chiness Valentine's Day

On the Chinese Valentine's Day, Love songs which
Pervade the horizon and Resound the blue sky,
Are supposed to be about love that lasts forever,
Forever and ever,
Forever and ever.

📖 情人像甜美的月亮

月亮很甜美
月亮很漂亮
情人很甜美
情人很漂亮
看到月亮
就想到情人
天空只有一個月亮
而世界有很多情人
一個月亮可以選擇很多情郎

📖 My Sweetheart Is Like the Beautiful Moon

The moon is sweet, and
The moon is pretty,
My sweetheart is sweet, and
My sweetheart is pretty.
Looking at the beautiful moon.
I would think of my sweetheart.
There is only one moon; yet,
There are a lot of lovers.
The moon can choose her own lovers.

📖 陳年的相思酒

陳年的相思酒
比茅台和威斯忌還強烈
喝一口
會流一串眼淚
喝一杯
會淚流成河
悲苦的陳年相思酒
含有濃濃的離別愛情和鄉愁

📖 Aged wine of Lovesickness

Aged wine of love sickness is
Stronger than either Maotai or Whisky.
Sipping it,
    one would shed tears like the flowing water in a river.
Bitter aged wine of lovesickness would make one think of
Parting love and feel sick of home.

📖 愛是花的芳香

愛是花的芳香
芳香洋溢在男女的心房
濃情蜜意,迴旋蕩漾
芳香瀰漫在親朋的臉上
其樂洋洋

芳香飄灑在敵人的手上
會使他放棄敵意的手槍
把酒歡唱

📖 Love is Like Flower's Fragrance

Love is like flowers' fragrance at the lovers' heart,
Full of affection and sweetness, swirting and nippting.
The fragrance would pervade the faces of relatives and friends
   Happily.

If the fragrance comes to the hands of the enemies,
The enmity between us
Would disappear.

📖 聽醉人的歌聲

你的歌聲,甜美迷人
你的歌聲,比美酒還醉人

聽醉人的歌聲
可以快樂開車
不是酒後開車

📖 Songs that Are Intoxicating

Your songs are sweet and charming.
Your songs are more intoxicating than wine.

Listening to the intoxicating songs,
One would drive a car happily.
It is not drunk driving.

📖 憂鬱的雲

天空有憂鬱的雲
而我內心有傷心的情
天空憂鬱的雲
可由日灑消散
而我傷心的情,纏繞綿延
久不離去
希望有一顆豔陽

在我心中,熊熊點燃
消除憂傷
給我快樂平安

📖 A Melancholic cloud

A melancholic cloud there is and
In me there is a broken heart.
The melancholic cloud could be
Dispersed by the sun.

I wish that there would be a burning sun
In my heart to drive away my sadness and
To give peace and happiness.

📖 彩雲追月

我的詩是華麗的彩雲
送給美麗的月亮
月亮是我的愛人
我夜夜追到天亮

華麗的彩雲
像開屏的雄孔雀
追求像月亮的雌孔雀

夜夜窮追
追到太陽升起
這是在天上遊玩的精彩愛情遊戲

📖 Colored Clouds Pursuing the Moon

My poems are colored clouds which
I dedicate to the beautiful moon.
The moon is my beloved who
I pursue till the dawn every night.

The colored clouds are like
The fully opened tail of a male phoenix
Pursuing a moon-like female phenix.

I ceaselessly pursue the moon till
Sunrise.
This is the most exciting game of love in the sky.

📖 彎彎的河流載著我的淚水

那彎彎的異鄉河流
像我故鄉的河流
載著我的鄉愁
載著我的淚水
載著父母的慈情愛意
載著親友的熱情蜜語
載著故鄉的泥土氣息

📖 The Curved River Carries My Tears.

The curved river in an alien place,

Like that in my hometown, carries my homesickness,

My tears,

My love to my kind parents,

My passion to my country folks,

And the earthiness of my hometown.

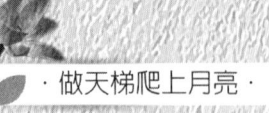

📖 做天梯爬上月亮

讓我們做一個天梯爬上月亮
不必太空船
不必太空站
不必做登月的夢想
就能登上月亮
可愛的天梯
由地球直達月亮
像坐高鐵一樣
直達幸福的天堂
並送月餅給月亮

📖 I Wish to Build a Ladder Leading to the Moon.

Let us build a ladder leading to the moon
Instead of a spaceship or
A space station.
We need not make it true in our dreams.
We would actually land the moon.
The lovable ladder would lead us from the earth to the moon
Like riding in a high speed train.
We would reach heaven which is full of bliss.
We would send sweet mooncakes to the moon.

📖 月亮守在妳的窗外

月亮守在妳的窗外
把我寫的詩傳達給妳
並傳達我的愛意
打開妳的心扉
使我們心心相許

📖 The Moon is Waiting Outside Your Window

The moon is guarding outside your window

And trying to give to you messages through my poems.

They are messages of my love to you.

I wish that they would please you and

That you would be my love.

流淚的飛蛾（一）

我是熊熊的蠟燭
妳是流淚的飛蛾
滿懷深情的淚蛾
是為了熔化濃濃的深情
化為天仙
在天上成雙結婚

📖 A Weeping Moth (I)

A weeping moth there is.
She is full of love.
She pounces on fire.
She tries to put out the fire with her tears.
She wants to devour the fire full of love.
She wants to hold the fire for her own forever.
The moth and the fire would never separate.

流淚的飛蛾（二）

一隻流淚的飛蛾
充滿全心的愛意
撲向煙火
要以淚水澆熄煙火
吞食充滿愛意的煙火
使這個煙火永遠屬於她自己
永不分離

📖 A Tearful Moth (II)

I am the flaming candle, and
You are the tearful moth.
The tearful moth is passionately flying
Toward the flaming candle
In order that you passion would melt down and
That you would become a fairy.
The burnt candle and the metamorphosed moth
Would become two in love in heaven.

📖 星星是我的眼睛

星星是我的眼睛
可以看透宇宙的奧秘
可以看透人生的意義

星星是我的眼睛
可以跟月亮甜言蜜語
可以跟藍雲遊玩嬉戲

星星是我的眼睛
多彩多姿
永遠美麗

📖 The Stars Are My Eyes

The stars are my eyes.
They could see the secret of the universe.
They could understand the meaning of life.

The stars are my eyes.
They could talk with the moon as people in love.
They can even play games with the blue sky.

The stars are my eyes.
Their life could be colorful.
Their life could be forever beautiful.

📖 我有兩支翅膀

我有兩支翅膀
一支飛到天上
一支潛入海底
都為了尋求宇宙的秘密
和探索詩的奧秘

📖 If I Had Two Wings

If I had two wings,
I would fly high in the sky with the one and
Swim in the sea with the other
To explore the secret of the universe and
That of poetry.

📖 哭泣的風

哭泣的風
在我耳邊響起
它吹起我懷鄉的盛情
它喚起我父母的思情

哭泣的風
在我耳邊響起
催促我要自強自立
不要流淚
不要悲戚
像太陽一樣
在天上快樂笑嘻嘻

The Weeping Wind

The weeping wind
Is ringing in my ears.
It reminds me of my homesickness and
My parents' love to me.

The weeping wind
Is ringing in my ears.
It urges me to be on my own,
Not to shed tears
Nor to be sad.
It encourages me to be like the sun
Smiling high in the sky.

📖 春天從大武山出發

春天從大武山出發
溫暖的元旦春陽
冉冉由太平洋昇起
照耀大武山
照耀台東海岸
照耀美麗的台灣
春天的腳步聲
由大武山開始踏響
　響徹雲霄
春陽舒展溫柔的雙臂
擁抱無限美好的希望
春天從大武山出發
給台灣發光
春意洋洋

📖 Spring Starts from Mount Dawu

Spring starts from Mount Dawu.
The warm spring sun on New Year's Day
Slowly rises from the Pacific Ocearn.
The sun shines on Mount Dawu,
On the coast along Taidong County, and
On the beautiful island of Taiwain.

The steps of spring resoundingly begin from Mount Dawu
Marching toward the clouds in the sky.
The spring sun extends her soft arms
To embrace boundless beautiful hopes.
The spring sun rises from Mount Dawu,
Giving light to Taiwan and spreading
Ambience of spring there.

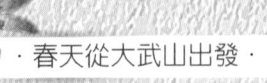

📖 春天從大武山出發

春天從大武山出發
熊熊的新年曙光
由太平洋點亮
照耀高高的大武山
像貝多芬的春之頌
給雄糾糾的大武山快樂溫暖
呼喚出台灣最早的春天
給台灣幸福平安

註：據氣象局說：元旦最早看到的曙光，不是在台東三台或高雄，而是在大武山頂上。

📖 Spring Starts from Mount Dawu

Spring starts from Mount Dawu.
The fiery dawn of New Year's Day
From the Pacific Ocean
Brightens the tall Mount Dawu
Like Beethoven's Song of Spring.
The dawn gives warmth and happiness to the majestic Mount Dawu and
Peace and bliss to the island of Taiwan.

Note: According to the Bureau of Meteorology, the earliest sunlight on New Year's Day appears at the summit of Mount Dawu, not at Sanxiantai, Taidong County, or Kaohsiung.

摘下月亮

摘下月亮
放在地球上
任人觀賞

摘下月亮
放在床上
任你親吻
任你撫摸
給你舒暢

摘下月亮
放在書桌上
把你的詩篇
放在月球上
傳給太陽
播放詩的光芒

📖 Picking the Moon

I wish to take the moon off from the sky and
Place her on earth
For people to see.

I wish to take the moon off from the sky and
Place her by my bed.
I could kiss her and
Embrace her.
I would feel comfortable with her.

I wish to take the moon off from the sky and
Place her by my desk.
I would like to write poems for her
To carry to the sun and
To help send their light to the universe.

📖 作者 · 沙白簡介

- 沙白,本名涂秀田,一九四四年生,台灣省屏東縣人。屏東初中,台北建國高中畢業,高雄醫學院畢業,日本國立東京大學研究。
- 沙白自幼年即習中國古典文學,青少年時,更吸取西洋文學和日本文學等,而成為融合中西文學思想的詩人。
- 曾任現代詩頁月刊主編,阿米巴詩社社長,南杏社長,笠詩社社務委員、心臟詩社社長、布穀鳥詩社同仁,高雄市文藝夏令營講師,亞洲詩人大會和世界詩人大會籌備委員。
- 曾應邀參加一九八六年漢城亞洲詩人大會,一九八八年台中亞洲詩人大會,和一九八八年第十屆曼谷世界詩人大會發表論文〈詩是現代社會最重要的空氣〉,獲大會極高評價,曼谷英文大報THE NATION(國民報),以首頁引介此文。一九九〇年長沙世界華文兒童文學會議,艾青作品國際學術研討會。
- 曾獲中華民國新詩學會詩運獎、高雄市詩歌創作獎、朗誦詩獎、高雄市文藝獎、中華民國兒童文學會獎入圍(第二名獎)、心臟詩獎、柔蘭獎、亞洲詩人大會感謝狀、高雄市牙醫師公會和中華民國牙醫師公會感謝獎、台灣文學家牛津獎候選人。
- 現任台一社發行人、《大海洋》詩社社長、中國文藝協會會員、中華民國新詩學會候補監事、世界詩人會會員、世界華人詩人協創會理事、高雄市兒童文學寫作學會理事長、六堆雜誌編委、中華民國牙醫師公會編委。
- 著作:詩集『河品』、詩集『太陽的流聲』、詩集『靈海』、中英文詩集『空洞的貝殼』(余光中、陳靖奇譯)、童詩集『星星亮晶晶』、『星星愛童詩』、童詩集『唱歌的河流』(中華民國兒童文學會獎入圍)、『沙白散

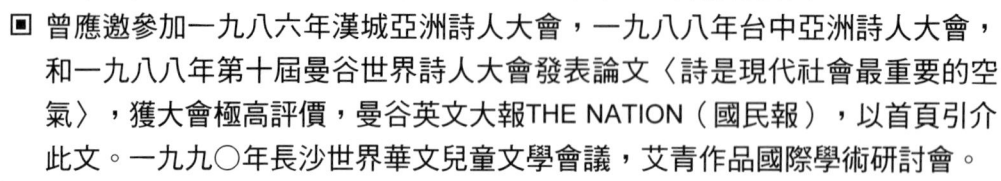

An Introduction to Tu Shiu-tien (Sar Po)

文集』、『沙白詩文集』、傳記『不死鳥田中角榮』、『毛澤東隱蹤之謎（補著）』、『牙科知識』、『快樂的牙齒』等，以及T.S艾略特和保羅、梵樂希等英日文學之翻譯和介紹。作品曾被翻譯為英、日、韓文等，在外國及中國大陸曾介紹過。

- 留美：哈佛大學、波士頓大學植牙中心。
- 中華民國口腔植體醫學會專科醫師、台灣牙醫植體醫學會專科醫師、國際口腔植牙專科醫師學會院士、前中華民國口腔植體醫學會監事及專科醫師甄審委員、美國矯正學會會員。
- 國際詩人獎、榮譽文學博士、ABI及IBC國際傑出名人獎、美國文化協會國際和平獎、台灣文學家牛津獎、中國文藝獎章；曾獲兩次國際植牙會議論文第二名獎、榮獲國際詩人協會國際詩人獎及卓越獎。
- 沙白詩作列入韓國慈山李相斐博士出版的「現代世界代表詩人選集」。
- 現職：台立牙科診所院長
- 住址：高雄市新興區仁愛一街228號
  　　　高雄市前金區中華三路135路
- 電話：886-7-2367603
  手機：0919-180875
- e-mail：shiutientu@gmail.com
  e-mail：taiyi.implant@msa.hinet.net
- 網址：www.taili-dentist.com.tw
- 郵政劃撥：04596534涂秀田帳戶

📖 An Introduction to Tu Shiu-tien (Sar Po)

Born on July 28, 1944 at Toulun Village, Zhutian Township, Pingdong County, Taiwan Province, Republic of China.

Education:

Zhutian Primary School, Pingdong;
Provincial Pingdong Middle School;
Jianguo High School, Taipei;
Department of Dentistry, Kaohsiung Medical College.

Foreign institutions where he pursued further studies and research:

Research Institute of Dentistry, National University of Tokyo;
Osaka University of Dentistry;
National University of Osaka;
Research Institute of Dentistry, Harvard University;
Center for Dental Implantation, Boston University.

Interests :

Chinese classics, Western literature, Japanese literature. Oriental and Occidental philosophy and Thoughts on the Arts and their theory.

Honors and Awards :

Award for Writing of Poetry, Kaohsiung.
Award for Chanting of Poetry, Kaohsiung.

Award for the Arts and Literature, Kaohsiung.

Roelan Award, Kaohsiung.

Award from the Society of Cardiology.

Award from the Republic of China Association of New Poetry.

Outstanding prizes from International Poets' Association, ABI (American Biographical Institute) and IBC (International Biographical Center).

Award from the International Society of Poets

A certificate of an academician in the Association of International Dental Implantation Specialists at the University of New York.

Honorary Degree of Doctor of Literature (Litt. D.)

Outstanding People of the 20th-century American Biographical Institute (ABI) and the International Biographical Center (IBC)

Award from the American Cultural Agency for Promotion of World Peace.

Second Award in the presentation of a paper at the International Congress of Oral Implantologists (ICOI), twice.

2004 International Peace Prize, for outstanding achievement to the good of society as a whole, by the authority of the United Cultural Convention sitting in the United States of America.

2005 as one of the Top 100 Writers in Poetry and Literature, witnessed by the Officers of the International Biographical Center at its Headquarters in Cambridge, England.

2005 Lifetime of Achievement One Hundred, signed at the Headquarter of the International Biographical Center of Cambridge, England.

Oxford Prize for Taiwanese Writers

Chinese Literature and Art Medal

Current Occupation :

Dentist, Taiyi Dental Clinic and Taiyi Dental Implantation Center.

Associations :

President, the Amoeba Poetical Association, Kaohsiung Medical College.

Editor-in-Chief, the *Modern Poetry Monthly,*

President, the *Nanxing Magazine,*

President, the Big Ocean Association of Poetry;

A committee member for general affairs, the *Li Journal of Poetry;*

A lecturer, Kaohsiung Summer Camp;

Associate convener, the section of poetry, Kaohsiung Qingxi Association of the Arts;

Supervisor, the Southern Branch, the Chinese Association of the Arts and Literature;

An editor, the *Liudui Magazine;*

A preparatory Committee Member, the Asian Poet Conference;

A committee member, the World Olympic Association of Poetry;

An academician, College of World Culture;

Honorary Doctor, World Conference of the Poets.

Classification of His Works:

Collections of Poetry:

Hepin (So. The Streams), Preface by Zhu Chendong, "The Realm of Poetry—

a Discussion of Sar Po's Poetry." Taipei: Modern Poetry Club, March 1966.

The Spiritual Sea. Kaohsiung: Taiyi She, September 1990.

The Hollow Shells, with Chinese and English texts, tr. by Yu Guangzhong and Ching-chi Chen. Kaohsiung: Taiyi She, December 1990.

The Streaming Voices of the Sun, in the Collection of Taiwanese Poets, #18, ed. the Li Journal of Poetry. Kaohsiung: Chunhui Publishing Co., November 2019.

Essays on His Poetics:

Sar Po's Essays on His Poetics. Kaohsiung: Chunhui Publishing Co., August 2020.

Prose:

Sar Po's Essays. Taipei: Linbai Publishing Co., September 1988.

Children's Literature:

「星星亮晶晶」 *Twinkle, Twinkle, Little Stars*. Kaohsiung: Taiyi She, October 1986.

「星星愛童詩」 *Stars Love Children's Poetry*. Kaohsiung: Taiyi She, September 1987.

「唱歌的河流」 *Singing Rivers*. Kaohsiung: Taiyi She, September 1990.

Biography :

An Undying Bird, Tanaka Kakuei (不死鳥田中角榮). (In serialization, Taiwan Times.) Tainan: Xibei Publishing Co., May 1984.

·作者·沙白簡介·

Books on Dental Hygiene :

Knowledge on Dentistry. Kaohsiung: Taiyi She, August 1987.

The Happy Teeth. Taizhong: The Commission of Education, Taiwan Provincial Government, April 1993.

Translation of Texts and Theories of literature, Taiwan and Overseas:

"T.S. Eliot, 'The Dirty Salvages' ", from English into Chinese, in Sar Po's Essays on His Poetics, pp. 256-273.

"Paul Valery's Literary Theory, One." in *Sar Po's Essays on His Poetics*, pp. 280-285.

"Paul Valery's Literary Theory, Two." in *Sar Po's Essays on His Poetics*, pp. 286-294.

"Paul Valery's Literary Theory, Three." in *Sar Po's Essays on His Poetics*, pp. 295-299.

"Paul Valery's Literary Theory, Four." in *Sar Po's Essays on His Poetics*, pp. 300-307.

"Paul Valery's Literary Theory, Five." in *Sar Po's Essays on His Poetics*, pp. 308-312.

"Paul Valery's Literary Theory, Six." in *Sar Po's Essays on His Poetics*, pp. 313-317.

"Paul Valery's Literary Theory, Seven." in *Sar Po's Essays on His Poetics*, pp. 318-325.

"On Something about Charles Baudelaire" by Kuritsu Norio, in *Sar Po's Essays on His Poetics*, pp. 326-336.

- An Introduction to Tu Shiu-tien (Sar Po)

"On Charles Baudelaire"
   by Kuritsu Norio, in *Sar Po's Essays on His Poetics*, pp. 337-350-349.

"On Charles Baudelaire and His Poetical Language"
   by Kuritsu Norio, in *Sar Po's Essays on His Poetics*, pp.350-360.

"On Charles Baudelaire and His Prose"
   by Kuritsu Norio, in *Sar Po's Essays on His Poetics*, pp. 361-370.

"On the Pains of Charles Baudelaire"
   by Kuritsu Norio, *in Sar Po's Essays on His Poetics*, pp. 371-374.

"On Rambo" by Kuritsu Norio,
   in Sar Po's Essays on His Poetics, pp. 375-382.

"A Dream Inside and Out, Two Poems,"
   by Shinkawa Kasue, *in Sar Po's Essays on His Poetics*, pp. 432-433.

"Two Poems by Yamamura Bocho,"
   in *Sar Po's Essays on His Poetics*, pp. 436-437.

"Some Ideas on Taiwan Poets"
   by Kaneko Hideo, in *Sar Po's Essays on His Poetics*, pp. 438-439.

"Kawada Kakuei, Mushanokoji Saneatsu, Chen Tingshi,"
   in *Sar Po's Essays on His Poetics*.

Papers Read in Conferences:

―――――――――――――――――――――――――――――

Papers read at the International Conference for Dental Implantation; Presented twice and awarded twice.

"Poetry Is the Most Important Air in Our Modern Society," read at the World Poets' Congress, Bangkok, Thailand, 1988; the speech was published in The Nation, Bangkok, Tailand.

📖 譯者 · 陳靖奇簡介

- 出生：台灣省雲林縣古坑鄉。
- 幼兒園：雲林縣斗六糖廠附設幼兒園。
- 國小：雲林縣古坑國民小學。
  　　　台北市西門國民小學。
- 初中：台北建國中學。
- 高中：台北成功中學。
- 學士：國立臺灣師範大學英語學系。
- 碩士：國立臺灣師範大學英語研究所。
- 博士：美國明尼蘇達大學美國研究所。
  重點研究：美國文學與文化，「二十世紀三零時代的美國左翼文學，普羅大眾與資本社會的矛盾等議題。」

- 經歷：
  台北市立景美女子高級中學英語科教師。
  私立大同工學院講師。
  國立高雄師範大學教授兼夜間部主任。
  國立高雄師範大學教授兼英語學系主任。
  國立高雄師範大學教授兼英語研究所所長。
  國立高雄師範大學教授兼文學院院長。
  國立空中大學高雄學習中心主任。
  私立和春技術學院教授兼副校長。
  私立致遠管理學院教授兼應用英語學系主任。

📖 Translated by Prof. Ching-chi Chen, Ph.d.

- Born at Gukeng, Yunlin, Taiwan, Republic of China.

Educated:

- B.A. and M.A., National Taiwan Normal University, majoring in English.
- Ph.D., University of Minnesota, U.S.A., majoring in American studies (social sciences about America and American literature).

Positions held:

- Professor of English, Department of English, National Kaohsiung Normal University.
- Chairperson, the Department of English, National Kaohsiung Normal University.
- Dean, College of the Liberal Arts, National Kaohsiung Normal University.
- Vice President, Hochun Institute of Technology at Daliao, Kaohsiung.

國家圖書館出版品預行編目(CIP)資料

盛開的詩花 = Flowers of Poetry are Blooming / 沙白著；陳靖奇譯. -- 高雄市 : 台一出版社, 2023.12
　面；　公分
中英對照

ISBN 978-626-95122-7-0 (平裝)

863.51　　　　　　　　112019332

盛開的詩花 (中英對照)

Flowers of Poetry are Blooming

著　　者：沙白 Sar Po

翻　　譯：陳靖奇 Ching-chi Chen, Ph.d.

發 行 人：涂秀田

出　　版：台一出版社

發 行 所：800高雄市新興區仁愛一街228號

電　　話：886-7-2367603; 886-9-19180875

印　　刷：德昌印刷廠股份有限公司

電　　話：886-7-3831238

郵政劃撥：04596534 涂秀田帳戶

出版日期：2023年12月 (中英對照)

Email：shiutientu@gmail.com

　　　　taiyi.implant@msa.hinet.net

定價新台幣500元(美金20元)

版權所有・翻印必究